ured out I had some spirits in my house, some that were there and could not leave or some that were just passing through.

So I started communicating with them. First, I tried the Ouija board, but I got nothing.

I bought a voice recorder so that I could try communicating with them. I would sit in a room that was active and ask questions like "What's your name?" or "Why are you hear?" I just wanted answers.

I had done some remodeling in my house, so in the laundry room that was recently done, that seemed to be a very active spot. I took my voice recorder into the room, shut off the light, and began to ask questions. After a few minutes, I caught a voice on my recorder. I was very excited, a voice I could not hear with my own ears, but with the help of my recorder.

I had asked the question "What's your name?" I repeated the question three times or so. Yes, I got a response: "Fuck you!" I was like, "Wow." I again asked the same question, and again I received the same response: "Fuck you!" It was then that I realized that the spirit was getting pissed at me for asking the same question over and over. So I apologized to the spirit and told it that I just wanted his or her name. So after my apology, I asked again, "What is your name please?" I did get a response. The spirit was that of a man, and his name was Jimmy. He would tell me of how he and a few others were trapped in my house. I had no idea what to say. I was speaking to an intelligent spirit, one that understood and could respond to my questions. At this time, I had five guests in my house.

These spirits must have been with the land the house sat upon. These were old souls trapped in time, wandering the earth and stuck in my house. I always felt watched and sometimes touched. It would be nothing to feel a cold breeze creep up and pass by. Things in the house would move, and the doors would open and shut on their own. Doorknobs would shake at will in the middle of the night and often during the day.

Shadows would dance on the walls; we could watch them run to and fro. Wandering souls would just pass through my house, sometimes wanting to talk. I started using a pendulum with a crystal to

A GUEST
IN MY
HOUSE

DAVID M. GUDDY JR.

PAGE PUBLISHING, INC.
New York, NY

First originally published by Page Publishing, Inc. 2015

ISBN 978-1-68139-751-1 (pbk)
ISBN 978-1-68139-752-8 (digital)

Printed in the United States of America
Cover art by Darrell M. Guddy

A wisp of a cold breeze brushes by me. I look for an open window or maybe a window that allows a draft to come through, but all are shut and tight. I have no idea or explanation of what is happening. This sort of thing would happen all through my house, and sometimes in the middle of the night, I would feel it pass over my bed. Door handles shake as if wanting to open, and then doors open on their own. I guess one would ask, What is happening, or am I losing my mind? Seeing things from the corner of my eye, I would ask, Is my mind playing a trick on me? Did I just see a shadow move across the wall? Voices that call my name and wake me up in the middle of the night—do they exist? Where is all this coming from? What would, or should, I do?

My first thoughts were, if they are talking to me, then I should be able to speak to them; they could hear me. I began just to speak out loud, telling them hello and asking them to leave.

Well, that wasn't working. I began to look to alternative means Ouija board, pendulums, all sorts of things. Then I discovered EVP (electronic voice phenomenon); this was a way that I could talk and communicate with whatever was in my house.

Sometimes the house was quiet; nothing was there it seemed but quiet meant trouble!

Shortly after a quiet spell, it would all start again. Out-of-body voices, things moving, things misplaced—all of which there we no explanation for. The cold breezes would start up again, and the time, there seemed to be a scent of perfume, something like a la would wear.

So it became a custom that when I would smell the perfume there was a woman's spirit or something present. By now, I had speak with the spirits in my house. Simple questions for the travelers. The plate has answers that the crystal will swing to. Yes, Maybe, No, and I will not answer—these are the words that they can answer with. Spirits, demons, all can use this method to communicate.

I started off with a friend experimenting with this…a little scary, speaking to the beyond. We would sit and ask questions and get responses. For a few nights, we were so wrapped up in this exciting new find of talking with the dead. This was so much better than using a Ouija board. Asking questions like "How old are you?" "Where from?" "How did you die?" "How long have you been at this house?" I was finding out that several spirits were trapped in my house and could not leave.

My house is very close to an old cemetery; spirits pass by and stop in. As we kept using the pendulum, we would get strong answers. This pendulum is a chain that has a crystal at the end, so it swings back and forth to the answer it desires. The chain would swing so hard at times, reaching a ninety-degree angle, and sometimes I would feel a hand on top of my hand, holding it and pressing down hard to the point that I would almost let go.

I still had my voice recorders with me, so I thought, why not try recording the sessions? So we started recording all the sessions on the recorder. We were very surprised at the results we received. We knew from before that we had spirits in my laundry room downstairs; we even knew some of their names. We prepared and were ready for anything to happen.

We set up and began to ask questions, but this time, we recorded everything. We called for Jimmy to come upstairs and speak with us. We asked the first question, and a female did respond. Her name was Sally, and she had been in the house for a long while. She began to tell us as we asked questions about her. She told us she was buried in the cemetery near my house; she had died in the late 1800s. She told us how she lived in this town when it was just beginning. She gave us her name and told us she was the only Sally that was listed in the cemetery. We then asked for her to call Jimmy up to us so we may speak to him.

With the recorder still running, we began to ask, "Jimmy, are you here?" and we asked a few other questions, hoping to catch an EVP response. After a few hours of asking questions and feeling the spirits move around the room, it was time to check our recorder. We went back and began to listen very closely. Spirits speak sometimes so softly and in a low tone that it is hard to hear them speak. Several voices came through, soft and in low tones, but there was a voice that stood out, very loud as if I were sitting right next to him. We asked the question, "Jimmy, are you here with us?" The response was amazing. He answered in a very normal tone, very laid-back, like no worries, and said, "Yeah…I'm here." This was so real and exciting to use, the voice recorder, as if it were a medium or a phone for us to talk and ask questions and for him to leave us a message.

We found some amazing facts about Sally after following up with what she said. My friend did the research, and she found out that what that spirit said was true. Sally was indeed the only Sally buried in that cemetery that was so close to my house. But why was she here, in my house, for so many decades, wandering the land and watching time go by, with no sense of time? Think about that. There were others that were there from the beginning of my purchase of the house, and they too had been unable to leave the grounds of the house. Was this a curse that they were stuck? I had another spirit tell me that he was indeed trapped, could not leave, so sad, unable to move on. I tried communicating with him from time to time. As far as appearance, making themselves visible, from time to time, I could see what I assumed was a person or maybe a shadow moving very quickly.

We would go back to using the recorder, attempting to catch an EVP throughout the house. We did get a few good EVPs, some that just wanted to say hi or talk to someone that was able to sense them and recognize that they were intelligent spirits. As we spoke to the spirits, we would find out that they love talking to those who can hear them or see them. A lot of the spirits were shocked that humans can hear and feel their presence.

My friend has the ability to see and hear the spirits (clairaudience and clairvoyance). A spirit came passing through one night. It was the spirit of a woman; she had died only a few years ago. My friend began to speak to this woman. The lady was shocked that my friend could feel, see, and hear her. When she came in the room, there was a smell of perfume…strong perfume. I could smell it so strong it was like she was in my lap. We asked her a few questions I think everybody that likes supernatural things and ghosts want to know. So we proceeded to ask a few unanswered questions. We asked how she traveled and if she could fly. "Are you stuck walking? What is the other side like?" I believe these questions are on everybody's minds. She did tell us how she gets around; she said she had been traveling for years, sometimes not knowing where she ends up, but she found a way to get where she wants to go. She would just think about where she wants to go, and she is there in a blink of an eye. The lady spoke of how she missed her children and family, so sad. She told us how she would go back to her house and see the kids and her husband but was totally unable to speak or do anything for them to realize she was there.

This spirit told us that she was passing through when she noticed a natural energy field in my backyard. She said it was five feet wide and stretched out from my laundry room all the way through my backyard.

My guest then was telling me, "This is why you have so many spirits in your house. They see and feel the natural energy field. It's like a gas station for all the spirits to come and refuel." Then she told us of thousands that walk the earth, that are afraid to travel to the light. So many are afraid of their destination…uncertain of their final destiny. She stayed with us for a while and told us of her travels, then told us that all the others knew that we can hear and see them.

I was beginning to feel I had a hotel, not a house. There were so many things happening and so many spirits to talk with, each with their own story and can talk forever about their lives and tell of their travels and the places they have been. It was interesting to listen with a sensitive approach.

As my interest piqued into the unknown, it all was becoming very interesting, like a drug. This was very addicting. Hearing voices, some out of the body, that were very clear. Hearing them answer questions as quickly as I hit Record. There was a very intelligent spirit responding. It became my hobby to try to speak with the dead each night. It wasn't hard to find spirits; they were all in my house.

One night I was at home with my friend, and a little girl came through. She was communicating with my friend. She was telling us of her travels. She had been walking the earth for a little over four years. She was trying to get home to see her mommy. The girl was approximately around nine years old. She was crying; sickness had taken her life four years ago. She didn't know that she could just think of a place that she wanted to go and be there. We had told her that we spoke to another spirit, and she told us traveling is as simple as thinking about where you wish to be. The young girl took the information we provided to her. She was all alone; no other spirits would speak with her. She had passed four years ago and was all alone.

I thought about this child, and it brought tears to my eyes, because this child had passed at such an early age and did not exactly know what was happening with her. All alone, she was wandering around in the spirit world. She was totally shocked that we could hear her and talk with her; no one had communicated with her ever.

Occasionally I would smell cigarette smoke. Where was this coming from? I didn't smoke, so where was it coming from? I took a walk around downstairs where I was at and found nothing, but yet the smoke was still in the air. Then as I was sitting on my couch, a cool breeze blew by me, smelling of the cigarette smoke. I had a visitor in my house. I figured it must have been a spirit in the house.

Another time I had the same thing happen, very similar to the smell of smoke. This time it was the smell of a woman's perfume… and quite strong it was. This time was a little different. I had felt a tingling sensation on my head, hands, and arms. This was a new sensation that I had never felt. I believe the spirit was touching me; she was making contact by touch. Then on my cheek, I could feel almost as if I were receiving a kiss. This was crazy and a little scary too. I sat as the sensations continued, not sure what to say or do. I could feel her presence very close. It was like a small electrical surge running through my entire body, something that I never felt before. The feeling of a person holding your hand, rubbing your arms, but then looking around, there was just me in the room.

I would also sometimes hear my name being called at different times throughout the house. Different voices would speak aloud so the human ear could hear without any aid. At night it would be the worst, like things dropping, and I would hear as if some things were actually moving. As I fall asleep, I would begin to drift off into a slumber then be woken by a voice calling my name. Was I crazy? I was sound asleep, and it's as if someone were in the room, calling my name. At times they would even tell me, "David, wake up." This would start happening in the early morning a lot, like three or four times a week, and that was just in the morning. During the evening, there was still activity, more out-of-body voices and noises that were unexplained. I guess the spirits love to talk to anyone, but when they can tell that you can see and hear them, that's when it really becomes interesting!

One evening, I was lying on my couch in my living room. I had a girl over and was wondering if the spirits in the house even noticed what was going on. She had come over to visit for a little while. Well, after a while, I decided to get my voice recorder out, just to see if I could catch anything. I had also just let my dogs out, so they were walking around. I press Record and asked, "Did you see that girl that just left?" I listened and got no response. So I asked another question. "Didn't you think she was pretty?" and to my surprise, I did get an intelligent response. The spirit came back with an amazing remark, very shocking; he said, "Yeah, pretty…pretty stupid!" When I heard that, you can only imagine my response. Here I was, talking to a not only intelligent spirit but one that can judge. How crazy is that?

The spirits were definitely paying attention, especially to details. As I kept asking questions to see what else I could catch, one of my dogs was acting up. My Rottweiler was getting on my last nerve, completely acting up, so while my recorder was still rolling, you hear me yelling at my dog, correcting him, then I played it back and was surprised at what I caught. When I played back my audio, I found a male's voice that came through so strong, like he was seriously pissed off.

After you hear me yelling and screaming at my Rottweiler, you can hear the spirit's voice very clearly telling me, "If you want to scare someone, scare me!" I was kind of terrified when I heard the angry spirit now yelling at me. This was different; I was getting scolded by a spirit for correcting my dog. I had to stop and take it all in, but to beat all, I heard my dog in a panting voice, saying, "Me scared…me scared…me scared…me scared!" It was now that I understood what the spirit was telling me. He had heard me yelling and correcting my dog, and my dog was telling him and me that he was scared. When I heard my dog speaking plainly about his fear of me, it made me feel like shit. I was so not expecting my dog to talk, but it was clear, and it was on my recorder, along with the spirit yelling and threatening me. When you get threats from the other side, it makes you stop and think…what exactly could this spirit do to me? This was an experience that I will never forget—my dog Gunnar speaking to me.

Another experience I had, I just got home from shopping and had a telephone on the floor. That was the type where it had a cradle and a long cord connecting the phone to its base. I had an answering machine in the corner of the room. I had some messages on it, so I went over and got all my messages. I proceeded to my kitchen. At that time, I had a landline phone mounted to the wall, and you had to look around the corner of the wall that was between the kitchen and my living room. Well, I picked up the phone to dial out and call back those that left me messages. The first call went through, and I spoke with the person I called, then I hung up and started to call the next person, when all of a sudden, the phone went to like a recording saying, "The number cannot be completed as dialed." I was like, what is going on? So I hung up the receiver and picked it back up. This time it was even weirder. I heard a tone…one like when the receiver is not hung up correctly. You know, it makes that strange sound that only happens when a phone is off the hook. I only had two phones, one in the kitchen, which I was on, and the other one in my living room. I looked around the corner, and there I saw that the corded phone was not only off the hook but also completely stretched out across my living room floor. Here was the problem: my living room phone was off the hook, but how? I was the only person in my house.

This was impossible. So I walked over to the phone and receiver. I picked up the receiver, and the mouthpiece on the receiver was still warm, as if someone was talking on that phone. I sat in the chair that was next to the phone, and it was then that I was getting cold bumps on my skin, and my skin was jumping with like an electrical current, like I was plugged in. It was then that I realized that there was a presence in my house, a spirit that I had seen move these things. There was no other answer for all this that had happened.

One night I was sleeping very soundly, but then that wonderful call to take a piss hit me, so I got up and proceeded to the bathroom. I walked out of my bedroom, then stepped into a hallway. I looked to my left, down the hallway into my living room, and there was an upright lamp that was on, and next to the lamp was a Coleman lantern (battery operated). The small Coleman was off, but my question was, how did the upright lamp get turned on? Well, anyway, I had to piss so bad I figured that I would just go turn the lamp off once I had relieved myself. So I made a right and went into my bathroom.

When I came out of the bathroom, I was looking straight down my hallway into the room with the lamp on, but this time, the upright lamp was off, and the small Coleman lantern was on. I felt chilly bumps run up and down my spine. I knew that I was taking a piss and no one else was here, so that means I had a spirit that could move things in my house. So I walked toward both lamps. As I walked that twenty feet or so, I was very scared, not knowing what to expect. After all, within that five minutes or so, a lamp was turned on and off and another was off then turned on. I was standing in front of both lamps, just staring at them, trying to grasp what had just happened. I did feel a presence that was with me in the room. I didn't do anything, but turn the small Coleman lantern off, turned around and walked down that hallway, and went straight back to bed.

So many times I have heard my name called out, mostly waking me up in the middle of the night or in the wee hours of the morning—calls such as "David...wake up" or just hearing my named called, "David." Then I would wake up and think, who is calling me? I thought at times it was a dead relative trying to communicate with me, but no matter where I lived, it seemed they found me or followed me.

I was renting a house in Cleveland with a girlfriend at the time. This house we stayed in was an older Cleveland home. We moved in, and I didn't really expect anything. I was wrong. It of course started out really small. She didn't believe in spirits or things of that nature. Well, it started off with us hearing our names called. She would be in our dining room on the computer, and I would be in bed, getting rested for the next day. Once again I heard my name called as plain as day. I was so positive that it was her needing something that I jumped up and ran into our dining room to see what she wanted. She looked at me like I was crazy. She told me that she did not call for me and to go back to bed.

On another occasion, we were both sleeping very good, then I woke up to hear a voice in my ear, calling my name, which woke me. A few nights later, she would hear her named called, so she came running to me, asking what I wanted. I then told her that I didn't call her, and she then told me it was my voice, no mistake. This was getting real creepy now. The spirit was mimicking my voice, making her believe that I called for her.

She liked to knit with yarn, and she had all the needles needed to do so. They were all in a little bag, so they were all kept together. Well, she would leave them out from time to time because she was working on a project. One time we got home, and she had left her needles out in plain sight, she thought. When she went to find the needles to knit with, she noticed that they were not there, so quickly she blamed me, that I had moved them.

She looked everywhere, everywhere in the open areas, because she knew that they were not put away. After looking everywhere, she finally went and looked in the container that had all the yarn in. It was there that she found the knitting needles very neatly tucked away properly, but no answers how they were placed there. She never wanted to admit that a spirit might have had something to do with all this. I was tired of all the nonsense and wanted answers, as anyone should. We had bought a digital camera, so I thought this would be a great tool to see if maybe we could see whom we were talking to. I had heard that you can capture spirits on a digital camera, so I thought, why not give it a try?

So one evening, I decided to try this out. I went into our bedroom. This was where all the voices had been coming from, so it seemed like a great place to start.

I walked into the bedroom that night and shut off all the lights and spoke out loud to the spirit. I suspected a girl or woman, because when I heard these voices, they seemed to be female.

With the lights off and the bedroom door shut, I began to take pictures. I took several all around the room, hoping to catch something. As I was taking the photos, I was speaking to her, asking her to show herself and that I meant no harm to her, just wanted to see her, because it was her voice I believe I was hearing. I finished taking the pictures, turned on the lights, and then went to the computer right away to see what was on my camera. I was so excited, and I was so hoping she appeared to me.

Once reviewing all the pictures that I took, there were two that stuck out. Here she was, standing right in front of me. Without a doubt, it was her, the one that had been talking to me. She let me catch her on my digital camera, finally evidence of what had been driving me mad. I would stare at the monitor's screen in disarray. I did believe, but it truly was hard to swallow. Here she was, with long hair and slender build. I was able to make out all her features very well. She was dressed as a maid, like early 1800s. Her dress had short sleeves with a white cuff (lacy); the same would be around her neck, a white lacy neck boarder. Her dress attire did indeed remind me of that of a maid. The dress itself looked to be black. She was a very beautiful young lady. I would guess her to be in her twenties. Finally a face and body to go with the voice that was haunting me. I had shown my findings to some people that were skeptics. They couldn't say much because the evidence was there in their face. I had a maid that was living with me at that time, a guest in my house. She never did anything that was annoying or anything that was real scary. It was always voices that we heard or small objects moved. I know sometimes you might never know who or what is haunting you. In this case, I was lucky that I caught the image with my camera. With this kind of evidence, how can you not believe?

It was now that I found a great tool to prove to people that spirits exist. I had captured a spirit on my digital camera. I did take other pictures throughout that house, and I found that there were many orbs in that house. I believe these orbs to be energy of spirits that could indeed appear if they have enough energy to do so. There were so many orbs, all in different sizes, some small and some the size of a basketball.

After all the pictures and voices, my girlfriend at that time still would have a hard time believing in these spirits, probably scared. Not too many people can take all this in and keep their sanity. I did have a dog at that time; his name was Max, a wonderful Rottweiler. This dog could see things also, like spirits moving through the house. I would watch Max watching all the activity, spirits moving around the room. Sometimes our television would just come on by itself for no reason and shut itself off also. Lights in the house also would flicker on and off at times, little things, never anything threatening to us. We lived in this house for two years.

Photography had become a way to establish truth and proof that these spirits did indeed exist. I started taking pictures just about everywhere I could. Orbs were everywhere. Each time that I took a picture, I was hoping to catch another apparition or something. I was getting pretty good at recognizing the presence of a spirit. I almost always would feel a cold breeze or smell a cologne or perfume that stood out from all other smells. There was also touching, which almost felt like a spider web going over your hand or arm, or an occasional kiss on the cheek, enough to drive you absolutely crazy. So if I walked into a room and felt like I had some spirits in the room, I would grab my camera and start snapping pictures like a madman. I would catch a lot of orbs and shadows, things I had no explanation for. The camera was great. It helped me explain what I was seeing, and I documented all the things that I saw.

When you walk into a room and see things moved around, I mean like nothing is where you left it, things rearranged, that is a little scary, 'cause you know that you left that there and that over there and so on. I think it is a game of moving things around, like a memory game, just to fuck with us. Countless times I have had things moved and made me believe that I had lost or misplaced them myself, which was very far from the truth. How annoying not finding your wallet or keys when you need them, looking around, wasting time because some spirits are in the corner, laughing about what they just did. Although I did find out that if I asked to find the missing items, that I was shown or told in some odd way.

I was amazed when I first bought my house. I was in an old community that settled in the 1800s. My house was only a young thirty years old at the time of purchase. I took pictures with my camera before I moved in and painted it. At the time I developed the pictures, there were so many orbs I thought that it was snowing in my house. Photos from every room proved to see orbs, all different sizes and would travel through the house. I didn't know what to make of all this; they're all kind of new to me. This did pique my interest in the paranormal, my own private investigation. Sometimes you could almost feel the heat of eyes on you or swear that you'd seen something moving from the corner of your eye, shadows moving quickly along the walls and ceilings—never had I seen or experienced all this activity. It was very exciting!

Once I had started the remodeling process, that was when everything kicked up to high gear. My girlfriend at that time was real fearful of the supernatural. She hated me talking or acknowledging the spirits that were present already. So if I paid no attention to them, they would just go away, maybe just disappear. That was not about to happen. As I told you earlier about my voice recorder, this was when I would use it to find that there were indeed a few trapped in my house. I started to use the camera to see if I could get them on film. Talking to them on the recorder was great, but I wanted more. I wanted to see just whom I was talking with. So curious I was it was driving me crazy. What did they look like? How were they dressed? So many questions that I so wanted answers to. I really couldn't talk to anyone about my new friends. I would be labeled as a crazy person. I just wondered how many people have guests that are with them but never speak of them for fear of being looked at as if they lost their marbles.

I'm sure there are some that have seen and heard or maybe just heard an EVP that sent chills down their spine—a voice that you have no explanation for. You asked the question to nothing you could physically see, but there it was, a real not-so-live voice, but a *voice*!

One day I walked into my house just as any other night, and as I walked into my kitchen, I could see a man walking in my living room. He was a tall fellow and was walking back and forth in my living room, and he never said a word.

My friend Faith and I went to dinner one night at a restaurant, and during the dinner, we both felt a strong energy between us. We thought it might be a spirit of some sort but never thought it would attach itself to us. When we got to our car and was sitting inside on the way home, we noticed the same energy. The spirit was riding with us in our car. We were able to communicate with the spirit; her name was Heather. She had only been dead for three years. She had been walking around and just hanging out. Well, she went home with us and immediately made herself at home. She was walking all around the house, checking things out, then she discovered the natural energy field in my backyard, where she met other spirits and then soon moved on.

On another occasion, I was walking in my house, and in my kitchen, I saw a man with a mustache sitting at my kitchen table. He had his arm and hand raised as if he were stretching, and he wore a hat, like an old gangster's hat. He had seemed to be following me around. This was not the first time that I had seen him in the house. I believe that he also had gone to work with me, because I remember seeing him watching me work, and one time when I was painting, he knocked my roller arm and a paint brush out of my hand to the floor. I was not for sure if this was the same man until I got home and saw him again; it was.

It is so not uncommon for people to pick up spirits and take them home. You could be shopping, grocery shopping, or out to dinner with family or friends. These spirits will just attach themselves to you, and you won't even know it until you are at home and strange things start to happen—things that you sometimes never paid much attention to before. So when things start getting misplaced and strange sounds start to happen, pay attention...you might have a guest. So many people have spirits in their house and probably don't even know it.

Because I have that natural energy field in my backyard, I get so many spirits that come through my house. I would say I have a sea of spirits or souls around my house, and they all love to talk. All have stories to tell, adventures all from the afterlife, which we all have questions about. If you could sit down with these spirits and ask questions, what would you ask? Let's say they come in and start talking. What would be the first question you might ask?

What was it like crossing over? Did you see your dead body as you left, and if so, what are your thoughts about that? Did you see the light, and if you did not go to it, then why not?

How do you travel ? and how fast? Are there limits on your travels? Can you leave earth? Do you see your loved ones often? Do you know what year this is, or do you keep any time? How do you sleep? Or do you sleep? Can you see other spirits? And can you speak with them? Can you see angels or demons? Do you haunt anyone or try to scare them? How many people can actually listen and hear you speak? Are you bored? What do you do or like to do to pass the time?

These are all questions you would love to find out. All the television shows and movies have the paranormal all wrong. There are evil spirits that will do you harm, but there are spirits that just want to talk and go about their business not bothering anyone. Most of them just love their families too much to abandon them. They feel they can offer guidance and watch over their kids and grandchildren. There are so many stories that can be told and can answer all and any question about the other side.

I was able to sit down with quite a few spirits (souls) and get their stories. Everyone was so eager to tell how they died and where they have been. It was quite interesting. For about two weeks, I would go into my backyard and ask for some spirits that wanted to tell me their stories. I have that energy field, so it was easy—just go outside and ask. I would speak aloud as I walked with my friend Faith. She is a great medium; she can actually listen and hear the spirits as they speak. She can also talk to them. So as I asked, "Who has a story to tell? I am writing a book, and I need some of you to share with me your experiences from the other side." I told them that I would publish their full name and the day and year that they died. I would give them the most respect and that all the living would love to hear their tales.

So it was very successful! I was able to gather about fifteen stories that are real. Everything that you have read so far and what is coming is very real. I have done my research with these spirits in asking them the most difficult questions to get answers. I know we all wonder what the other side is like or what is to be expected. We don't know, but after reading these stories that are coming up, you will have a very good understanding of the other side.

You will be surprised to know all spirits can smell. Most that I have spoken with all prefer the smell of coffee. I guess that is one thing that they miss. One evening, Faith and I were wrapping up our session with a spirit, and we had a spirit pop in on us because Faith had made some popcorn, and she smelled it all the way in my backyard. So we told her she could stay as long as she gave us her story about her afterlife. She did give us a great interview as she sat and smelled the fresh popcorn. I thought this was amazing. For a spirit to come in and tell us how much she missed the popcorn, it was a great talk. You will read about it.

So all the things that go bump in the night might not be so bad. It might just be a relative or a close friend checking up on you and maybe even protecting you. It is just crazy how many spirits told me that they are staying earthbound just to watch over and protect their loved ones.

Just keep in mind that the stories you are about to read are real and from real people like you and me. They just have passed on and wanted to share all the answers with us. I think you will be shocked at their stories.

Steven J. Thomas died at the young age of forty-five, from Seattle, Washington. His son is currently living in Ohio; that is why Steven is here. I asked Steven to give me his story and be a guest in my house, to tell us all about things we don't know or understand. So here is his story.

> My name is Steven J. Thomas. My son is Thomas Steven Thomas; he is twenty-seven now. I died at age forty-five. I was from Seattle. My job there was a democratic mediator. My job details were

to hire people to get money for their party and work with local politicians and people to find out what their needs were. I helped take care of the changing of office to make sure it went smoothly. I was doing this job for twenty years before my death. My wife died one month after our son was born; her name was Isabelle.

My death was brought on because I was not paying attention to my son. I was just so caught up in my work, so my son got heavily involved into drugs and got his girlfriend pregnant. I thought that I did wrong and was blaming myself for my son's screwup.

My son and his girlfriend got into a car accident. They both were drunk, and she was pregnant, so I didn't hear the full report, so I thought that the baby had died. So I went home, feeling all to blame, and hung myself in my living room. I had left a note for my son, explaining my death and how I felt. My son still has the note, and he reads it every day I see him.

I didn't cross over because I can't leave my son. I need to watch over him and my grandchild. I passed away on September 2, 2003. When I passed, there was a light for me. I could see my wife, my mother, and a friend. My wife had reached out and touched me. I told her I'm not coming; I need to stay with my son. My wife nodded and let go. The white light followed me for two days, and then it was gone. I can see other spirits and talk to them. I do speak to many, but only a few will talk back to me.

It is interesting how fast I can get from one place to another. I just close my eyes, and in a couple of minutes, I can be anywhere that I have been. It takes me longer to travel where I haven't been. I made it to Egypt in twenty minutes from Ohio, at my son's house. Many spirits just walk aimlessly around, not knowing how to travel. I do keep up with time and what day it is. I also keep up on current events.

Many spirits are evil, and they try to do harm to people. Once, I chased an evil spirit out of my granddaughter's room. The evil spirit was moving things and talking to her and making her toys come at her in a scary way.

I do miss the ability of taste, but I can smell anything.

I do have a lesson that I have learned in life by me. It is that other people are more important than yourself!

While talking to this spirit, I felt his pain as he took his life because he thought that he messed up his own son's life. The suicide that was committed was a very strong way of showing his remorse and his attempt at forgiveness.

I was looking for a younger spirit to speak with, and I found a young lady by the name of Tiffany. She was only seven years old. She has a very interesting story to tell about her life. She sat down with me and told me of her experiences and troubles, so here is her story.

My name is Tiffany Trenton; I passed away about one year ago. I am from a small town just outside of Pittsburgh. I was seven years old when I passed on. My family and I died all together. It was dark out, and the roads were bad. It had been snowing, so the roads were very icy. It was wintertime and just a few weeks before Easter in 2011. We were coming home from a church event, when our car went off the road and hit a tree. Before I knew it, all things had changed. I was different. I'd seen the light but did not go to it because I was looking for my mom and my brother. So I started to walk to see if I could find them. I have been walking around, looking for them, following lights, and trying to find the light that they are in. Because the light that I saw didn't have anyone that I knew, or recognized the hand reaching out to me.

I walk a lot, and sometimes I sit and close my eyes, and when I open them, I am somewhere else. I often wake up in my bedroom, but someone else is living there now.

I can talk to other spirits, and I follow them a lot. Most spirits won't talk back to me. Some are scary, and some will tell me to do bad things to people. Like one time, a spirit wanted me to go under a car and cut things to do harm. Another time, I was in a house playing, and the evil spirit wanted me to start a fire.

When I died, I was really scared. Now I am not so scared, but lonely...

Not too many people that can hear me are nice to me. They will not talk to me or help me find what I'm looking for. Kids that can see me throw things at me, and if a child tells their parents they can see me, the parents don't believe them. I had a little girl that could see me that I stayed with for a while. She would tell her mom about me and point at me. So the mother kind of made a game out of me, where the child pointed at me, the mother would try to grab me.

I do have the ability to smell. I can smell flowers and things in the air. I did spend a lot of time playing in fields with the flowers. I saw a coyote kill a deer once, so I hid in a tree for a week.

I would love to find my family and have them close to me.

When we were done speaking to this very young child, we gave her an opportunity to go into the light. My medium Faith was able to create the light in which this little girl went into gladly. She was reunited with the family that she had been searching for all this time.

It felt so good to help this young wandering soul. Now she wanders no more.

Now as I was looking for my next guest to talk with, this young man came up to me and asked if I wanted to hear his story. So he came into my house and began to tell a very interesting story about his lie and his afterlife. His name was Adam Greenburgh, and he began to tell me about himself.

> I was twenty-seven years old when I passed on July 19, 1922. I was in the hospital, sick with TB. I came from a very wealthy family, but no matter how much money we had, it still couldn't help me. When I died, I didn't go to the light because I wanted to stay around and torture my sister, because she got everything and I got nothing when our parents died. She screwed up everything, the money and the business. She wouldn't listen to our parents; she would not act right.
>
> Upon my deathbed, as I was passing, Lucifer appeared unto me. He had chosen me to be a demon. Because I believed in hell, when I died, Lucifer grabbed me, and He told me, "I can make you more, and what would you like to do?" So I chose to be a demon for Lucifer. I do many things for him, and I also get a lot of free time to do what I want to.
>
> I have possessed and killed for Lucifer. I can make people do things without their knowledge and harm themselves and others. I have made a girl slit her wrists and would possess by going through their mind. I can make people steal, cheat, and lie. I can travel in an instant, but I can't go through dimensions.
>
> I try to influence other spirits to do bad things to other people, to be spooky and scare them. I have to keep track of some of the spirits whenever I am told.

I followed Grace Kelly and helped destroy her. I took her away from Hollywood and her family and made her life a secret hell. I caused her so much physical pain every day.

I also helped some robbers rob my family bank, First Peoples Bank. They took the vault.

I come and go, and I do small things to famous people and politicians. I influence the things they say. When they talk, they think that they are speaking, but I intervene and make them say something that they didn't intend to say.

Sometimes I wish that I did not take Satan's offer. I have a hundred-year contract with Satan, so I do whatever Satan tells me to do. After one hundred years, I will finally be free from Satan's bidding.

Satan came to me himself while I was dying, and I made a decision to be with and to do as he asked. He told me that I could be on earth and take care of anything else that I wanted. There are many that are like me, keeping track of earth-bound spirits.

If I could tell the living one thing, it would be, people, do not make deals with Satan. It always goes wrong no matter what life you are in.After speaking with Adam, I was very enlightened. I had no idea that a dying spirit could become a demon. The afterlife he chose seemed to be that of regret, and nothing seemed to be what it was. I know he did and still does a lot of Lucifer's bidding. He is still under contract until the year 2022.

I came across a young boy that had passed from cancer. He had a very touching story, as he tells it.

My name is Jamie Blackburn. I died in August of 2005. I had cancer, bone marrow cancer. I started going to the hospital when I was ten years old. It took them a long time to figure out what was wrong with me. I was in and out of the hospital for six years. I would be in the hospital for three or four months at a time. While I was in the hospital, it was better than being at home, because I had friends in the hospital that were sick like me. We always played special games and got special food. At home, there was just my mom.

I was on a lot of drugs, so I felt very little pain. At my time of dying, my mom and friends were all at my side. When I passed, I thought that I'd seen a very bright light with my dad in it. I did not realize that I was dying. I thought that I was having a dream, because I had many crazy dreams before.

As far as travel, I just think where I need to be, and I am there. I have come across many bad spirits that I have met. I had a crazy lady try to take me places that were not nice. She took me into a burning building and said, "Watch them die!" because she had started the fire. The way that I traveled with her was that I stepped into her energy, and she took me with her. We traveled as one. Sometimes I travel in cars with people. I always want to drive.

I have been into many churches, trying to figure out what to do with my decisions about the light. I didn't realize what it was for. I do wonder why so many spirits have not gone into it. Sometimes I see the same spirits in passing. I do have some advice for the living: be sure of where you are going when you die! When I was done speaking to Jamie, I felt so bad about his condition and his great need to go to the light. I could clearly see that he was a tired soul, tired of traveling and so sad he missed the light, because he thought that it was a dream. So I had my medium present, and we asked Jamie at the end of his story if he would like to go to the light. He was so happy and excited that once Faith created the light, he ran into it. So now Jamie is at rest with all the rest of his loved ones and not wandering the earth.

My name is Marybeth. I was eighty-seven years old when I passed away. I am from Sioux City, Montana. I went to sleep one night and just didn't wake up. I did see the light, but just didn't want to go. I was a schoolteacher. I taught fourth-grade kids and taught many Indian children. I was married for thirty-five years before my husband passed away, and I have four children who are all alive. I did go to my own funeral and heard many people talking about me. I was surprised that I did not hear anything bad about me. I was very happy that everyone missed my cooking.

When I want to travel, I just close my eyes, and I am where I want to be. I went to Egypt, to the Great Pyramids to visit. I was able to get inside of them. Those people must have been very small people. I'd seen brilliant drawings on the walls and felt a lot of energy. I have also been to Australia. I could touch the wildlife. It was amazing because I was able to touch things now that I couldn't touch while I was alive, like poisonous things, snakes, spiders, and birds.

I have met up with other spirits, and we would visit different places together. I met up with a spirit in Russia, a guy, and we traveled to different places. I have been to Finland, and I skied and climbed mountains. I have been to Fashion Week in Milan, Italy. I was able to get backstage, and I saw the models popping a lot of pills. I have been to Alaska to see the polar bears, and I spent the night in an igloo. I go and visit my

children often; they are doing well. I have been
dead for about twelve years now, and I am having
more fun now than I ever did when I was alive!

Marybeth is quite a traveler and loves the other side. It seems
like now she is enjoying her afterlife. She has met a number of people
and made me understand that she was very happy with being able
to travel.

I find it amazing that all the spirits have so many things in
common. They all have a very good sense of smell. I have had some
of these spirits that ask for coffee. Almost all wish they could have
a cup of Joe, so they know that they can only now enjoy that fresh
scent that we all enjoy also, but we can drink it. Popcorn is another
smell that the spirits love. I guess, all food; it reminds them of their
lives. I can understand the burning of incense. The smell goes a long
way, and it comes in so many different smells, all of which the other
side loves. Even the smell of some good scotch will go a long way.
Alcohol is another thing that the spirits miss, the smell of all the
different liquors.

Well, my medium Faith and I were sitting at my table, eating
popcorn. The smell was so delicious it filled the room. I guess it
had traveled outside and a little farther, because as we were eating
the fresh popcorn, a spirit came in and asked to stay and smell the
popcorn. We were amazed that the smell went so far and brought in
a spirit. So I told the spirit she could stay if she would share her story
with us, so she agreed but made sure she could smell the popcorn.
Well, we began to speak with her, and this is her story.

> I'm Cindy, and I was twenty-one years old when
> I passed away. My boyfriend had been cleaning
> his guns, so as he was cleaning them, one of them
> accidently went off. The bullet had gone through
> my side. I died at the house within minutes. I saw
> his eyes, and that was the last thing that I'd seen.
> I didn't want to believe that I was dead. I saw
> my body lying there in front of me, and I didn't
> know what to do. Then I saw the light, and I was
> so confused. It all happened so fast to me. I was

unsure of what to do. I did not want to leave my boyfriend; he was crying so hard.

So an ambulance came and tried to bring me back to life. When they got there, they assumed it wasn't an accident. My boyfriend did tell them it was an accident, but the police didn't believe him, so he convinced them to bring in a medium to prove his innocence. Once the medium arrived, I was able to tell my story to the medium and convinced them of his innocence.

My funeral was very sad, lots of people crying, and there were people that I didn't even know. People spoke things, and they exaggerated all of what happened. My sister spoke at my funeral and lied. She made me out to be more than what I was. Many people didn't believe that it was an accident, so they said bad things about my boyfriend. One lady that was there said I deserved what I got for being with him.

When I want to travel, I just speak to myself where I want to go, and I'm there. Sometimes I end up places where I don't want to be. If I have not been there, it is harder for me to get there.

I was surprised that I can still hear people talking, and even more that some people can hear me talk. I stayed out of the light so that I can watch over my family and friends. Many spirits stay behind to watch over all their loved ones.

So sad that this girl lost her life at such an early age, only twenty-one. I was very happy to speak with her and share my popcorn!

I had bought a mirror from a yard sale one summer; we barely used the mirror. My girlfriend at the time was driving around and spotted the mirror. It was in excellent condition, so I bought it for twenty dollars. We took it home and placed it in an empty bedroom, where it was left all alone. So some time had passed, like a year or so. The mirror, of course, needed some attention, like a good wipe with some glass cleaner, so it just so happened that my friend Faith, the medium, was wiping the mirror, when she heard a voice say, "Ouch!" She looked around for someone or a spirit in the room with her, but she saw no one. She rubbed the mirror again and began cleaning it. Once again, she heard, "Ouch!" At this time, she realized the mirror was talking. Faith then began to address the mirror, "Are you talking?" Then the mirror began to explain and tell her what happened.

Faith immediately came and got me. This was crazy. This woman was trapped in a mirror. A witch had placed a spell on her and trapped her in the mirror. I had an idea, and I told the spirit in the mirror that I would get her out. She didn't believe me. Well, I had been practicing some magic with spells and writing my own spells. I had a wand to cast with, so I grabbed my wand and went to the mirror and said a spell in English to release her from the mirror. I did cast that spell directly at the mirror…nothing. I heard the woman in the mirror say, "You are not strong enough to break the spell. You are weak." Upon hearing her tell me that, I was now determined to get her out of that mirror cell. I thought for a moment, then I realized that if the spell was in Latin, then it would be stronger. So I took my wand in hand, and I began to say the spell three times in Latin, "Referri non tenet sed est hoc anima!" which, translated in English, is, "Mirror no longer hold but free this soul!" After saying these words three times and delivering a powerful energy to the mirror, demanding her release, a light shot off the mirror. It looked like a star. The woman was released, and she was standing in the room, holding on to Faith for dear life. She had been trapped for twelve years in the mirror, and now she's free. So we asked her name, and she responded with, "Katherine Dubi." Now I was asking her for her story. I knew it must have been very intense and exciting, a chance for her to walk me through everything that had happened to her. She did agree to sit and speak to me. She was still in disbelief that she was out of the mirror after twelve years. She would keep holding on to Faith, my medium, and staying very close to her. Being free, this was all new to her. I can't imagine being trapped in her situation for such a long time.

So now you will hear her story as it happened to her as she tells it—a very interesting one!

My name is Katherine Dubi. I was placed in a stand-up mirror by a witch. Now let me explain how I got here. I used to grow things like herbs and other things that the witch wanted, so I told her that she couldn't have anything else from me without paying. The witch stole things from me. One day, I caught her and confronted her about it. She told me, if she couldn't have anything else from me, that she would place a spell on me, and that was the last time that I'd seen the lady. It was a couple of weeks later that when I looked into the mirror, and I thought how much better looking I was than the witch. I was looking in the mirror, then the next thing I know, I dropped dead, and my soul was captured in the mirror. It seemed like a while before the police arrived. They found my body in front of the mirror where I died. I cried, and I tried to talk and scream for the police to hear me.

I was in the mirror for a while before it moved. I was moved to storage, then someone came to storage and got me and took me home. I was taken to a big house, and I was placed into a large bathroom with a changing area. I was there for a few years, then the mirror was sold. I then went to another house. I didn't like it much there, too many people touching me. They didn't know that it was hurting me when they touched me.

Then I was sold to David at a yard sale. When I got to David's' house, I was placed into a bedroom where I would stay for about one year. I enjoyed being left alone. I could only see any-one that passed in front of me. So a girl in this house started to rub me, and I felt pain. That's when I screamed, "Ouch!" The girl heard me yell then told her boyfriend about it that night. He approached the mirror and began talking to me. I didn't respond. I just wanted to be left alone.

Then the next thing that I know, he is trying to pull me out of the mirror. He had a wand and cast a spell to release me. As soon as the spell was cast, I was instantly released from the mirror's grips. I felt like I was tossed out and was completely scared and terrified because I was trapped in that mirror for twelve years. I was a guest in David's house, and very glad to be! It was he who released me. I was from Medina, Ohio. I would tell everyone that reads this, don't fuck with witches! What an incredible story about the woman trapped in the mirror. I had to help her, because if I were trapped in a mirror, I would want someone to help me out also. I was just glad I knew what to do. It was an experience that I will never forget! I had a spirit approach me in my yard. He and his wife had died together and did not go into the light. They were afraid because each had their own light. They didn't want to get split up and lose each other. So he wanted to speak with me, but she didn't. It was a few days after I first spoke to him that he came into my house by himself and asked if I would write his story.

As we sat at my kitchen table, he began to tell me about himself.

I'm Tom Burgerson. I'm from Chicago. I was a factory worker for many years. I died at age sixty-two. My wife and I were in a car accident involving a semitruck. We died together on the scene. At the time of my passing, I did see my mother trying to get me to go to the light and go with her. I would have gone to my mom, but my wife's spirit came to me for help, so I stayed.

She had told me that she didn't want to go into the light. She was afraid. She wanted to keep a close eye on her child. We both died about three years ago [2009]. We stayed and watched our son, and then we watched our grandson be born. My wife insists on seeing our grandchild constantly.

When we travel, we walk or take a bus, so me and my wife can stay together. We did try to travel by simply thinking about where we wanted to be, but when we tried that, we became separated. So now if we travel separate, we agree to meet back at our son's house.

I've see an evil spirit one time enter a bus we were on. He had started pushing people around and taking things, so we got off the bus. We don't encounter too many evil spirits.

I have scared people that I didn't like when I was alive, and I have also tried to move things. I still prefer to sleep, habit or not. It feels better to get some rest. Me and my wife usually travel to hotels and sleep. We would sleep in the empty suites. We also sleep at our son's house. We always do what she wants to do. It never changes.

Christians believe that once they die, they go straight to heaven or hell, but you have a choice to stay on earth until judgment day. During our stay, we travel the earth. We watch over our families and get to see the world. We are restricted to only travel the ground. We can't fly at all by plane, because it travels up to the first heaven. It is funny to watch some spirits that think they can get on a plane, because once they get on, when the plane starts to climb, we watch the spirits fall right out of the plane back to the ground. Spirits are not to fly.

If I could give a message to all the living and what I have learned from my life and on the other side, I would say, have no regrets. It does no good on the other side. Tom was a great spirit to talk to. When we were speaking to him, he was wanting to smell some scotch. He said he missed the taste, but he could smell it. So I just happened to have a bottle. I opened it, and he was able to enjoy a long smell of scotch. We were only able to talk with Tom because his wife didn't want to speak to me.

I met this young boy who was in a tragic accident. He was only twelve when he passed, and now you get to hear what he had to tell me.

I am Calvin Thomason. I was only twelve years of age when I passed away. I was in a bad farming accident that happened in the evening. I'm from Wooster, Ohio. My family owned cattle and farms. I would help out on our farms.

President Roosevelt was in office during my time. I do remember the Great Depression. My family helped out during these hard times. We would have a line every morning to receive food. My mom would cook, and they all would get food, a basket, and potatoes to go. We would give small quantities of milk out for babies, and Mom also made soup and mush to give out. Dad would rotate helpers on the farm so that everyone had some money. It was only me and my little brother at home.

When I died, I was with a farmhand. I was trying to fix something on the plow, but the farmhand didn't see me and ran me over with the plow. There was a lot of blood. I was injured on the side of my body and my arm. I was carried into the house. My mother was screaming and crying. I remember seeing angels; they were floating all around my body. Then I remember my mom lying across me, crying while I was still alive. When I passed on, she closed my eyes. I did reach and touched the light. I saw my grandfather in the light but stayed behind to look after my mom. The light was with me for four days. I did stay with my mom for a couple of days, then wandered away.

When I travel, I walk mostly, but I have closed my eyes and thought of places that I would like to go, then I would be there. I have come across some evil spirits that try to get me to hurt other people. Most of them are mean and tell me to go away. I have followed spirits around and also have sat and talked to some spirits for a while, but no friends.

I can smell things. I love to smell apple pie. I like to sleep at night when I can find a nice place. I thought that I would go straight to heaven. I wish I would have. I am so tired of traveling and wandering around.

At this time, my medium Faith and I offered Calvin an opportunity to go to the light, because Faith can produce the light he needed to follow. We spoke to him, and he agreed to go to the light. Once the light was created for him, Faith saw his mother coming to greet him as he ran to her. We were so happy to reunite the mother that so missed her boy and help the boy that was wandering the earth for years.

The next conversation was a little disturbing and sad. I had this spirit that wanted to talk to me but gave me a fictitious name. He did not want his real name said. This boy's mom had killed him, and he wanted to tell me about it.

Call me Joe. I died on December 12, 2010. I was seventeen years old when my mom strangled me in my sleep. My mom was going crazy. She was a schizophrenic. She used to hit me and call me names. I had a padlock on my bedroom door. I would lock myself in my room at night, to keep her away from me. The night that she killed me, she was hiding in my room. She waited until I was asleep, then she strangled me and killed me. She called the police and confessed her crime.

She used a scarf to strangle me. The police took her away, and then she went to trial. The case was dismissed due to her illness, and she was put away.

I travel around, telling other spirits my story. I ask them, "What would you have done?" They tell me they would haunt their mother as well, but some say not to bother her. She will go to hell. I still haunt her every night and torture her for what she did to me.

I travel sometimes to places I don't know, just to get away from it all. My favorite places to go are dance clubs. I like to watch all the women. I dance with them, but they don't know it. Sometimes I would follow them home. I would sit in their room, watch them, and sometimes I would play with them and touch them.

Once there was a lady getting ready to jump off a very high bridge. I saw her and went to her and whispered in her ear. "Don't jump! Don't jump!" and she didn't jump. I like to go swimming in the river down south. Sometimes I would go stay at my grandparents' house for three weeks at a time.

If I could tell all the living one thing, do not trust anybody! Joe will forever torture his mother for what she did. How could any woman want to kill their son? This was such a tragedy.

I was fifty-four years old when I died. My name is Elizabeth Thomas. I died on May 20, 1980. I was a seamstress since I was sixteen years old. I worked out of my house. I was married for a while but couldn't have any children. I grew up in a family of five. My mother and father both passed away before I did. I don't know what happened to my other siblings.

I made doll clothes, wedding dresses, bridesmaid dresses, and I would make uniforms for the girls, like cheerleading, prom, and dance dresses.

I passed away from cancer, ovarian cancer. I had it for five years from when I found out.

They cut me open and took out my ovaries and uterus. After that, my cancer spread throughout my body. I had stopped going to the doctors and went on with my life. So eventually I died. The doctors would come to my house because I wouldn't go to them.

The last thing that I sewed was a wedding dress for my friend's daughter Mary.

When I died, I did see the light, and I reached out to touch it with my hand, but it was cold. I thought about going into it many times before it disappeared. After the light went away, I felt very sad. I didn't know where to go. I started to encounter other spirits. I would follow the other spirits around and talk to them. Many would just tell me to go away. I have also come across some evil spirits. They are demanding and scream in my face, telling me to go scare people and to hurt people and do bad things.

Not too many spirits stay with me long. One time I had a child that stayed with me for a couple of years, and one day she just disappeared. I did have fun with this little girl. I would take her shopping, and we would pretend that we could buy everything. We would play in the fields and smell the flowers. We would also go to the zoo and pet all the animals. It was fun having someone with me, but very lonely and sad when I don't. I don't like being by myself all the time.

I enjoy summer when I can smell things, like the trees and flowers. There is a house that I visit. It has a rose garden. I spend a lot of time there in the summer.

When I travel, I walk most of the time. I closed my eyes one time and thought about the rose garden that I always visit, so I did end up there, but I was scared because I did not understand the way or how it worked. I do miss the smell of the bakery near my house and getting fresh hot doughnuts with tea.

My faith was strong. I read the Bible every day. My favorite story in the Bible was the wedding, when Jesus turned the water into wine. I didn't go to church every week, although I tried. I went to my funeral, and it was good. All the people were sad and crying. I was surprised my sister came up from Florida. I hadn't talked to her in a very long time.

Well, if I could give a message out to the living, it would be to be happy every day and not be sad. My medium Faith created the light for Elizabeth. So after many years of wandering around the earth and being lonely, she was finally going to the light. So she stepped into the light, where she was no longer alone!

It always bothers me to speak with a young child, because it seems they were cheated out of life. So many years that should have been lived out, but somehow they were cheated out of those precious years. I have spoken to a lot of children, and it is always interesting to hear their stories. So next is a young child that will tell us his story as he lived it.

I was eight years old when I passed away. My name is Sam Zefers. I am from Philadelphia. My life at home was fun. I learned a lot. I was homeschooled, but I wanted to go to school to play with all the kids. My mom would make learning unique and interesting. I would get to go to the library during the day. I would pick out a children's book, and my mother would make me read the book, and then we would find something in the library that was a fact about the book and research it further. We would often visit museums and historical places to learn things.

I got sick with pneumonia at eight years of age, and the antibiotics didn't work. I was coughing a lot. I was put in the hospital and hooked up to some kind of machine, and I remember seeing my parents there every day, crying at my side. I died one day that my parents were sitting by my side, then the next thing that I knew, I was standing behind them. I was screaming at them and trying to touch them, but they didn't hear me. I also tried jumping up and down, and I tried pushing them, but none of it worked. A nurse came into the room and told my parents, "I'm so sorry, he passed away."

I did see the light, but I didn't know what it was. The light followed me for four days, and it disappeared after they put me into the ground. I followed my parents home that night, and I got to sleep in my bed. I slept in my bed every night until they moved, and I stayed with my mom every night until she died. I did see her in her passing, although she didn't see me. She went to the light. I didn't know what to do after that, so I just started walking. I figured that I would try to find my grandfather's farm, and still have not found it yet.

I have run into many spirits that have tried to help me find the farm. Scary spirits try to make me go with them to people's houses to scare them. They also want me to play with little children and have them do bad things. Many times they tell me that I am going to hell. They try to tell me that I am an evil child. I stay away from them now. If I see one, I turn and go the other way. I will not talk to them.

If I could tell the living one thing, drink your orange juice. My medium once again created the light for this young boy. She watched him as he walked into the light where his grandmother met him, and he no longer walks alone.

I was thirty-two years old when I died in 1939. My name is Joann Broma. I'm from Indiana. I used to pick vegetables on a farm and cook for the family, and I also kept watch over the children. I was basically their housemaid. I was never married and had no children.

I once had a lover. He worked on the farm. He took care of all the animals. He was very tall and strong with dark black hair. We had a secret relationship for seven years. He had moved on two years before I passed away.

When I was taking care of the children, I had the most fun. Their daughter was the oldest child, Melisa, whom I became friends with. I taught Melisa how to cook and sew. She taught me how to read. She would read to me from her schoolbooks. I also taught her about plants and flowers, things you can eat and things you can't.

I grew up in Indiana with my two brothers. My family was very poor. I left home at ten years old, and nobody came after me. I stayed with an old black lady. That is where I learned how to cook and garden. I stayed with her until I was thirteen years old. When I got there, there was another housemaid that showed me how to run the household. I worked for this family until I died.

When I saw the light, there was a man in it that scared me. I didn't know who he was. He was in my light for two days. I stayed on the farm for a while, waiting for someone to come get me. I thought that God would come get me. Another spirit came by the farm and spoke to me about death, the spiritual world, and traveling. She said I could walk anywhere that I wanted, or I could just think about someplace that I wanted to go, but I didn't know of too many places to go, so I traveled to the Statue of Liberty and the Alamo. I hung out in Texas for a while. It was very different, then I went back to the farm where I used to stay.

I had a friend that heard that there were people here talking to the spirits, and that some of the spirits that go in don't leave. So they are curious about the people that come in and don't leave. These spirits know that you are taking their stories about their lives. The spirits say that you are unique. Not too many people can talk to the spirits.

There are some children that I came across that could see me and tried to touch me, but I could not talk to them. One little girl was reaching to touch me. She wanted to tell me something, but her mom pulled her away as the little girl cried out, "The lady! The lady!"

My funeral was a small service, then I was buried on the family's farm.

If I could give the living a message it would be, play more with the children. Their innocence can make your day better and take away your worries. Joann asked my medium at this time to create the light so she could go home and cease wandering the earth.

The next person I spoke with had a very touching story. This was a strong spirit while he was alive, and it carried through into his afterlife. I really don't think people change much from here to there. We all carry the same spirit through.

I'm Kevin. I passed away when I was forty-four years old. I am from Chicago, and I was a brick layer for about twenty years. My father was a drunk and used to beat me, so I used to hide in the cabinet under the TV. I would get into the cabinet when it was light outside, then come out when it was dark. Sometimes I would hide under my bed, where my mom would find me. I had one younger sister. My father was a very bad man. When my sister turned thirteen, he used to fuck her. This lasted not more than one year before I took her and left. We came to Ohio, just me and my sister. I was only sixteen at that time. So I met up with a friend, who let us live in his house. My sister went to school, and I started working. I took care of her and made her see a doctor. The doctor helped her not scream at night, and with time, she started to be more social.

When I turned eighteen, we moved into our own place, and she continued to go to school and started working as well. I took very good care of her, and I didn't allow her to date until she was eighteen years old and out of school. I made her go to college. She got a grant and got to go for free. She is now a nurse and married with children, and I watch over her very closely.

I was in a car accident in Pennsylvania. The car went over a cliff; the road conditions were very icy. I was furious when I died. All that I could think about was who will watch over my little sister. I wasn't ready to go. I had more things that I wanted to do. I didn't want to miss my niece's sixth birthday. I saw the light. My mother was there. I told her that I didn't want to be anywhere she was. The light followed me for three days. I think that it is sad that you can wander around and see people and not be able to interact. It is torture. The only good for me is that I can see my sister and that she is okay. My sister did cry a lot when I passed away.

I came across a group of evil spirits one time. They told me they were going to hurt me. They were going to make me go blind, because they wanted me to kill someone for them. I told them that spirits can't hurt each other like humans. These spirits followed me around for some time. I had to go far away.

Kevin did want to leave a message for all of us, he said. It is that one's actions speak louder than one's words. Kevin didn't want to go to the light because he wanted to continue looking after his sister and her family.

What a strong man, even at age sixteen, to take his sister out of an unbearable situation, move to a new state, and make a life. His sister has to be very proud of him.

My name is Kristine Marie. I died at six years of age. I lived in a big pretty house, and my bedroom was pink, pink everywhere, pink walls and a pink bed. My dad was an attorney, and my mom stayed home and took care of me. We lived in Avon Lake, Ohio.

I like to dance. I went to dance school. I always wore pink. I played piano, and I was just starting out, so we had a music room in the house. Once a week a lady would come to my house and give me piano lessons.

I also liked to play with dolls. I liked to change their clothes. They had lots of outfits. I would line them all up against the wall and teach them notes.

I went to church every Sunday, but I didn't pay attention. Instead I played with my toys. I did believe in Jesus, and I liked to sing.

When I died, I was sick, so my mom kept giving me medicine, but one morning, I didn't wake up. I stood watching my mom shake me. I cried, "Mommy, Mommy, I am here!" I watched as they came and took my body away. I just sat in the corner with all my dolls, crying. My dad came home and sat on my bed, just crying all night. That was the most time that he had ever spent in my room. I stayed in my room until Christmas. I left after Christmas because I couldn't stay and watch my mom cry anymore. I went to Christmas Mass with my parents, and I stayed at the church after they left. Some spirits came into the church. They were old people. They explained to me how I could travel to get away from everything. They told me to close my eyes and think about a place that I wanted to go. So I closed my eyes, not actually believing that I would go anywhere.

The first place I went to was Paris, France. I went to the Eiffel Tower and just walked around Paris. I did stay in Paris for a while and enjoyed smelling all the pastries. Now I knew that I could travel anywhere, but first, I wanted to see if I could go back home in my bedroom, and I was there. So then I decided to visit all the places in the books that I could remember. I went to London. I rode on the big buses. I got to go into the Big Ben Tower that no one else can get into. Every time that I traveled someplace different, I would always go back home.

Kristine loved to travel once she figured it out but was always certain to go back home. I guess she felt a sense of security in her old bedroom. I guess we never really lose that.

Another little girl passed away so tragically, as you will read her story. I spoke with so many young children that had passed away. It was so sad to hear these stories as only a child could tell. Lucy was only nine years old when she lost her life. Now she will tell you her story.

My name is Lucy. I passed away when I was nine years old. I liked being at home. My mom died when I was born. I just had my daddy and my stepmom. My stepmom didn't arrive until I was seven years old. I took jazz class since I was three. I liked to watch TV, although I wasn't allowed to watch much TV. I was the only child. I just wish I had a brother or a sister. I'm from Kentucky, just outside of Lexington. We had a horse farm, but I didn't like the horses. We had hundreds of them.

I had friends that would come over my house, where we would hang out and play. I had an in-ground swimming pool with a diving board. My friends liked swimming in my pool. We would have pool parties and order pizza. My dad worked a lot but stayed home. My care keeper was Kelly. She was like my mom and my friend. She taught me how to be a girl, and she shopped with me. Kelly took me to New York for a shopping weekend just before I died.

I liked summer camp. I would go for two weeks every year. I liked meeting new people at the camp, all from different states and countries. The camp was in San Diego. Every year we would take a tour of the city.

I died October of 1999, just before Halloween. I had already picked out my costume. I was to be Aerial. I had gone horseback riding with my two friends. They begged for me to go even though I didn't want to. I rode the horse that I knew, Bell, but I hadn't ridden her for a while. We went riding up some hills, nothing steep, up to our lake from the farm. One of my friend's horses wanted to go farther than we wanted to go, so I rode my horse very fast to get to my friend's horse. The next thing that I knew, I fell off my horse and died. I saw my body, and my friends around my body. I looked up, and all

I saw was white everywhere. I saw a light come out of the white. It was my mom. My mom told me to come with her, so I turned and I looked at my friends, and they were all crying over me. I told my mom to wait while I went and spoke to all my friends. I tried talking to my friends, but they couldn't hear me. When I turned back to the light, it was still there, but my mom was gone. I didn't know what to do, so I went back to the farm. I saw my father and Kelly running over to my body, so then I went into my room and stayed there. Kelly came into my room a few days later, crying. I tried talking to Kelly, but she couldn't hear me.

At first I didn't think I could go anywhere else. So one day, I'm sitting in my room with my eyes closed. I was just thinking about how much fun summer camp was, then the next thing I know, I was there. Once I realized what I did, I tried to go other places that I have never been to before, so I tried that, and it worked. I went to London, where I rode boats on the river and where I visited all the fancy shops. I did meet another spirit in London. This spirit was from the United States. We traveled back to New York together. She was from New York, so I got to see where she lived. With her help, she and I traveled by bus and car. Then we traveled back to my place to show her where I grew up. We stayed there for a little while, then we left and traveled to Missouri, where we would visit a friend of hers, then we traveled more. We met a girl once. She wanted us to push people at a store. We also came across two boys that wanted us to help break windows in people's cars and throw things at them. We laughed at them and ran away.

If I could tell the living one thing, a message that I have learned, it would be, don't do anything that you really don't want to do! We were able to create the light for this little girl who earlier had missed her light. My medium Faith told her she would create the same light that she had seen when she died. The light was then created, and Faith was able to see Lucy run into the light, where her mother was there to greet her. After all these years of missing her mom and crying, the light was in front of her, and another opportunity for her to go to heaven and be with her mom.

After speaking with all these younger spirits, we had an older gentleman come in my house. He was eighty-seven. He had lived a full life, a very nice person and spirit. He had a story that he wanted to share with us, so here it is.

I was eighty-seven when I passed away. My name is Ron. I'm from West Virginia. I come from a family of twelve living and three that passed. We were all poor. We would work the coal mines. I was born and died in the same house. I was the oldest boy, and I followed in my father's footsteps. The rest of my siblings, except one girl, moved away. Most of them didn't move too far. A couple did move to Nevada. I met my wife when I was sixteen years old. We got married when she turned seventeen years old. She was very pretty; her eyes sparkled. We had three children, two boys and one girl. I was a worker in the mines. I liked to play chess. I beat everybody I played.

I died in my rocking chair. It was my time. I passed away in June of 1992, right after I paid all my bills!

I saw the light. My mom and my wife were standing in it. I asked my wife, "What ya doing in there?" because my wife didn't like my mom. My wife said, "You have to come with us." I said, "Hell no!" I didn't want to be around them. The light followed me for a couple of days. I was glad not to see my mom and my wife in the light the last two days. I wasn't sure if the light would even go away, but it did after they put me in the ground. It was then that I started to wander around.

When I travel, I walk, sometimes fast, sometimes slow. I had followed some friends to your field. To be in the energy field is equal to a very good night's rest.

I did go to church twice a week. I was a good man.

My message to all the living is, live simple, and don't complicate things. Walking the earth for so many years was wearing on Ron. We asked him if he wanted to go to the light. He was a good man and should deserve to go to heaven, and he chose to do so. So Faith created the light where Ron stepped into the light as he told us good-bye.

I passed away at age eighteen. My name is Zach Huth. I grew up in a small house in Cincinnati, Ohio, and I had one sister. My mom had a miscarriage, and she went a little crazy from that, and my dad worked at a factory. My dad would play ball with me a lot. I really loved it.

Every summer we would go to the parks and zoos. We also would travel to Louisville, Kentucky, for family reunions in the summer. I really loved summer. It was a chance to get away. I was not very good in school. My parents always made me stay home and study. When I got to high school, I played football. I had to study hard to play. Before I died, I was looking forward to going to college.

I overdosed on drugs, which caused my death. So here is what happened. I was at a party, and there were all kinds of drugs present. I tried a little of everything, and some a little too much. I believe it was too much crack cocaine that killed me. There were some older kids at this party, with much more powerful drugs. They had the crack. I started out smoking it, then it became a game of who could do more than the other person. I had done so much that I fell over and passed out. They were all pointing at me and laughing, then I realized that I was standing there, looking at my body also. I was looking at my friends in disbelief. I was yelling at them, telling them to stop. I was staring around the room and noticed the light. I saw my grandfather in the light. He said nothing that I could hear. I wanted to help my friends to stop taking drugs, so I didn't go into the light. I really wanted to apologize to my parents, because I knew that I had broken their heart. So I went back home and lay on my bed for a while. I would follow my mom around for days. I did go to my funeral, and there was a long line. Many people that I didn't even know were there. People were saying how much that they missed me and how much that they liked me. Some were lying because they didn't even know me. It was a very long funeral. I was surprised at all the flowers, because I was a boy.

I found another spirit at the funeral home. This spirit had been around for a while and would come and visit this funeral home often. This spirit taught me how to travel, simply by closing my eyes and then going wherever that I wanted to go. The first place I traveled to was Disney World. I went there and stayed there for a long time. My parents could never afford for us to go when I was alive. Then I hit up most of the major cities in the United States.

I like to stay around my friends and watch over my friends. Scary spirits will try to get me to do bad things. They want me to hurt people and start electrical fires in their homes.

It was the summer of 1974 when I died.

If I could tell the living one thing, don't do drugs. I would still be alive if I had not done them.It was such a pleasure creating the light for this young boy. He had made some bad decisions, one that cost him his life, but now he is where he belongs, a better place. After walking the earth for over thirty some years, he is at rest.

My name is Jenny Ligue. I passed away when I was twenty-four years old. I'm from Kankakee, Illinois, and I died on May 16, 1990. I grew up with Mom and one sister. I went to school there, and I was a cheerleader. I ran track in high school, and I always wanted to be a doctor. My mom discouraged me because we didn't have enough money, but I was very determined to be a doctor, so I applied at Ohio State and got accepted. I worked as a stripper for money to help me through school and made damn good money. It paid for my schooling, my car, and the place that I stayed. I partied a lot down there the first four years, then I started my doctorate program. I was constantly working. One day I collapsed at work [the hospital]. They didn't know what was wrong with me. They put me into a coma. I was in the coma for about one month. They discovered rare small tumors on my brain. When I came out of the coma, they suggested different treatments I could take, but as a medical student, I knew the side effects. I also knew the statistics that nothing would work. My estimated time to live was six months.

I quit school and took a trip to Paris. I spent three weeks in Paris. I'd seen everything. I ate a lot of good food and had a lot of fun. Then I moved back home to see my mom. I stayed with my mom till the end. I died six weeks after I arrived at my mom's house. When I died, I saw this big beautiful light. I really wanted to go into it. It was very warm and inviting, but I was afraid of the unknown and uncertain, so I did not go. The light followed me around for three days. So I stayed behind to see what else I could do. I thought that I could help people.

I traveled back to Ohio State and to the hospital where I was an intern at. It was there that I met up with other spirits. They taught me how to travel. They told me that I could just think about any place and I could go. The first place that I went was India. After India, I was done with the other countries, so I came back to the United States, where I went back to my mom's house. I travel back and forth from my mom's house to the hospital. I usually pick up other spirits at the hospital. That's when they told me about this energy field. They described the energy field to me and that it lasts a lot longer than sucking up energy any place else. This field is rare and rich with energy.

I went to my own funeral. All my friends and family were there. I heard all the people talking about me. It was a very nice funeral. I was surprised at how many people from Ohio State University came to see me.

Well, if I could tell the living one thing as a message, it would be, the other side is not as interesting as you might think, but it is also not as scary either. Jenny continues to travel, wandering the earth. I can't believe how many lost spirits

are just walking around. Some like to check in on
family and friends and to make sure all is good.

I do have this energy field in my backyard, and it is all natural. This field attracts spirits from all over, and to my amazement, they all talk to one another. So many spirits that I have spoke with seem to have heard about me and my medium and know that I am writing this book. They actually tell me that they heard that some spirits don't leave the house once they walk in. In this case, we have had spirits that we have sent to the light they missed when they died. So yes, they walk in, and some don't leave the way they came in, but choose to go to the light. Every night the field in my yard is full with spirits, so it is real easy. Just to walk out and start talking and asking who wants their story told. I usually don't have a problem with getting them to come in my house, sit down, and talk of their past and afterlife. I have met so many spirits and found out through these interviews about the afterlife that I didn't know. This has truly been an education process about those that have passed on. Each spirit still carries his or her own personality still. They can laugh, smell, see, and travel. Emotions are still very much alive on the other side. So many souls still love and care about those who still live. They try so hard to get the attention of us who still live. They really do try to communicate with us, but many of us just don't pay attention to them.

In speaking to so many, I do find out things that some of the others would not talk of. I was just speaking to a spirit of a woman. She was at my table, and there was a napkin just sitting there. I asked her to move the napkin, raise it up, or just move it around for me. She then told me, to my surprise, that it was against the rules to do such a thing. I said, "What?" She repeated that it was against the rules. Then I began to ask her what the rules were. What she told me, I had never heard before and never thought of it.

She did begin to explain, "First, we can never move things in front of people. Second, we can only move things in front of children under the age of five. We can't become one with the living's body, and we cannot kill."

I then asked her, "When did you find all this out?"

She answered to me, "When I died, there was the light, but there also was a person, maybe an angel, who spoke to me. He told me, if I was not going into the light and if I was staying on earth, then these are the rules that I must abide by."

I had no idea about this at all. She was the first to tell me these things. It truly is a gift to be able to communicate with those who have passed on. We all can learn so much just by listening.

I walk into my kitchen and find a couple of spirits waiting to talk with me and a few more in my living room. They have all heard that we can hear them. Many come in disbelief and must see and hear for themselves, and they have also heard that I am writing a book about all their stories, past and present. It is to a point where I almost have a little gathering in my house, all waiting their turn to speak with me. It is really a treat to speak with all those that have passed on, and I am privileged to deliver their stories to you.

> I died on February 19, 1969. I was forty years old, from Tallahassee, Florida. I grew up in a small white house, very pretty and very decorated. I was the only child, and my father was a vet. My father made no time for me. My mom baked a lot. She would bake for the church, funerals, parties, and just for fun. I do miss the taste of all my mom's homemade pies. I miss her strawberry pie the most.
>
> I liked going to church and school. My school was next to the church. The church would have dances for the young people. Everybody would come. I liked to go swimming in the lakes and in the pools. I had an aunt that had a swimming pool. They were very wealthy. I liked to play games outside, like croquette and badminton. I was married and had two children, a boy and a girl. I stayed home and took care of my children, and I baked like my mom, and I helped my mom bake. I taught my children everything that I could. I took my kids to church and made sure that they knew God. I loved my life, my kids, my husband, and all the simple things.

I had gotten very ill. I had a fever that they could not control. I also had an infection that they couldn't find, then I died. I was lying in my bed, sick for about one month, then I passed away. When I passed, I saw the light, a bright round circle about the size of a window. I didn't go into the light because I needed to stay and watch over my children.

I met a guy in Atlanta, Georgia. He wanted me to come with him to a building. Inside the building, he had a stash of things that he had taken from people. He wanted me to help him collect this junk. I told him that I didn't have time for something so stupid. I told him no, so he got very mad and screamed at me. He told me good luck with my life.

I went to visit my own grave, and a very creepy, scary thing came chasing me, so I left the cemetery and have not been back since.

I learned how to travel on my own after I died. I wanted to visit my sister, and I was thinking so strongly about her that I ended up at her house. I realized that if I thought really hard, I could end up there. So I visited some places that I have been. I liked the ocean a lot.

I find it interesting that you can hear me. I get tired a lot, so I sleep. I like big pretty beds, and I like big houses. I have visited Graceland, and the inside is not as pretty as I had hoped.

If I could give the living a message, it would be to laugh every day. It makes things easier. Rachel decided to go to the light and saw her mom there to greet her. She also had been tired of traveling this earth and wandering without reason.

The next spirit had been wandering around for quite some time. I will let him tell his story. It is very interesting.

My name is Jeremiah Lee. I passed away in 1715. It was very cold outside. My family migrated from Baltimore. They came on a ship from England. My family was given land in the Missouri territory at that time. My family settled there when I was five years old. We built our home not too far from another family that came across also. The other family's name was the Hayes. We farmed the land, and we all helped each other. We lived by a small stream, where we would get our water from. After a small quarrel with the natives, we were able to use the lake. The natives helped us learn how to hunt and fish. They also let us know what else we could eat on the land, like nuts and berries. Once we had farmed the land, we would give the natives food for helping us. After we were there one year, my mom had a baby. It died two days after it was born. My mother was never the same after the loss of that child. My mom taught me how to read and taught the two children from the other family also. The mother from the Hayes family taught us math. When I got older, I would learn for a few hours a day, then go work in the fields.

When I was about fifteen years old, I met a girl. She was fifteen as well. Her family had settled not far away. They had moved down from Ottawa, Canada. I tried to court her for a long time, and finally she accepted. We were married in the spring, and all the families in the area helped build my house so we would have it before winter. My wife and I had a baby the following summer. We named her Sarah. She was beautiful like my wife. I went about farming and taking care of my family for quite some time. When I was about twenty, there was a fight. A different Indian tribe came on our land and tried to move us out. Because my wife was very scared, she had convinced me to move to Ottawa. Her grand-parents were there, so we moved there. It was a very long journey. Since she moved down here from Ottawa, she knew the best route to take to avoid trouble. We arrived at her grandparents' house just before winter. The trip from Missouri to Ottawa, Canada, took us about three months. We stayed with her grandparents until spring. Then we bought a house on squatter's rights. My wife had our second child. It was a boy. We named him Jeremiah and used her father's middle name, George. I got a job at the mill, where we would get the wood ready to make furniture.

I was very sick one winter. I was having trouble breathing. The doctors gave me medicine, but it didn't help. My wife out and got a local medicine man. He came and made me tea, which helped me breathe better. The Indian man said that if I did not get better in two days, then I would never get better. That night, my wife sat next to me all night, crying, and in the morning, I was dead. I saw my body lying there, and my wife was still sleeping. I tried to touch her, to comfort her while she was still sleeping. I didn't want to wake her up and have her scream. I saw the light, and my mom was talking to me, telling me to come to the light. I told her no. I had to make sure my wife was okay. When my wife woke up, she didn't scream. She stood up after she touched my body and saw that it was cold. She then walked out of the room and then walked outside and screamed very, very loud. She then fell down to the ground and lay there in the snow, crying. The doctor came to the house and found her in the snow. Then the doctor brought her in the house and warmed her up. I sat with her many, many days and watched her cry. I stayed and helped in my way to watch the children and help take care of the place, and I stayed with her until she died.

After my wife died, I wanted to go back to Missouri to see if the house was still there. I started out just walking there, but then I ran into some other spirits that told me if I thought really hard about where I wanted to go, I would get there. So I thought about my home in Missouri, and I was there. Then I went back to Baltimore, where my family arrived. I stayed at the harbor, picturing my ship arriving as a boy. The Revolutionary War had been started. I'd seen soldiers in the area. They were having a war, and I didn't like it, so I left. I met a woman spirit. She went with me back to Ottawa. I told her all about my wife and how she died. The woman stayed with me for a very long time. She took me to New York, where we got to see the country, hills, and things. She took me back to her country, Ireland. We stayed there for a while and played. We liked to visit ancient area caves.

In Ottawa, the spirits of the natives would gather in a certain spot. It was interesting in the way the natives carried on their traditions in the afterlife. If you tried to talk to them, they thought that you were interrupting their lives, so they would say mean things, like "Your spirit will not make it to the skies." If I could leave a message for the living, it would be, traveling when you are dead is much easier than when you are alive. After 297 years of travel, Jeremiah was asked if he wanted to go to the light if we created it for him. So he decided he had enough of traveling, and he entered into the light, which my medium Faith had created for him.

This was the oldest spirit by far that we have come across, a very gentle man and tired of traveling. He had seen so much and lived three lifetimes. It was crazy the way that he approached Faith and me. He told us he heard about two people in Ohio that can talk to the spirits. He said, "I didn't believe it, so I had to come and tell my story. I'm so glad that I came." He told us he was just amazed that we could hear him speak, and he was very anxious to give us his story. It was hard to believe that he traveled so many years—297 to be exact!

I am Rich Cotter. I was ninety-two when I passed away. I died in June of 1982. I was born in a hospital, and my mom gave me up to her friends, because my mom was only fifteen years old. I was raised by Judy, my mom's friend, and they had a little boy. They were very nice people. They didn't have lots of money, but they weren't poor. I went to school and church on a regular routine. There was always a chart of what was to be done every day. If all were done, everything was smooth. We weren't allowed to question them at all.

I remembered a happy time when I got a bike for my birthday. It was a good time in my life that summer. When I turned thirteen years old, they made me work. I started at the mill cleaning, cleaning up after people. I worked at the mill until I was eighteen years old, then I enlisted in the army. I never left the base in Michigan. I met a gal. She was a nurse on the base. Her name was Cassandra. We got married when I was done with my service. She wanted to stay where she was from, but I convinced her to come to Cincinnati. I had a job back at the mill that I was offered, so we moved back there. We bought a small house near my work, so I could walk if I needed to. My wife was pregnant a couple of weeks after we moved back. She gave birth to a little girl, Anna. We ended up having three more children, so a total of four. As of now, only two live. My wife died two years before I died. I never knew what to do after my wife died. I went to her grave every night, and I apologized for all the bad things that I did. I only hope that she hears me. I still visit her grave every night.

I went to bed one night and simply didn't wake. So when I passed, I stood up and saw my body lying there in bed. Then I saw the light but didn't go, because I was afraid of it. I was not sure of where I would go. The light stayed with me three days, then the light went away after they placed my body in the ground.

When I travel, I just close my eyes and think about going to where I want. The farthest I have traveled was to California to see my daughter. I usually stay in and about the Cincinnati area. I heard about your energy field from the other spirits. We have a group called the Spiritual Book Club. We talk of gossip and what is going on. It is made up of people who are friendly and want to chat. Because you can hear the spirits, they speak of you amongst themselves. The spirits say that you are writing a book about stories which are told by the spirits. Some spirits didn't believe us when we say that someone can hear them, so I wanted to come and see for myself, if it were true, and it was very true, as I sit at your table with you and talk to you as a guest in your house.

Rich did decide to go to the light in which he was before so afraid. I spoke to him and assured him he had nothing to worry about, but to go to the light and be with his wife. He was traveling every night back to Cincinnati to visit and talk to his wife at her grave. I told him she was not there. She had gone to the light. I told him he was wasting his time visiting every night. It was just easing his mind. What he really had to do was to face his fear of the light and just go into it and be with his wife, so he did at the end of our wonderful conversation.

I am amazed how much the spirit world has taken notice to me getting stories from all the spirits. All these stories are true and really being told from the souls that lived that life. These are the spirits that were afraid of the light or just missed it and were trying to figure out how to get back to the opportunity to go to the light. My medium Faith has sent so many of our guests to the light. The word has spread throughout the spirit community that we can create the light they once missed. So many spirits now just come in my house and ask to speak to us. They want to tell their story and get another chance to get to go into the light. The energy field is very popular with the spirits. They come from all over, then they hear that there are two people in the house that can really hear them. This is what gets their attention. I think the spirits want to talk to the living. It's just that our ears are not tuned in to them. So many times we talk to our dead loved ones, believing that they can hear us, and they can, but it is they who are really trying to get you to hear what they have to say. So next time you are speaking to your passed loved ones, just remember to listen very closely, because I assure you, they are talking to you and trying to communicate. Just listen very close.

Just thirty-two years old when I passed away in the early summer of 1987. My name is Sarah Maltine. I grew up in Louisville, Kentucky. I lived in an apartment with my mother and younger brother. My mom was a waitress, so I raised my brother because my mom worked constantly. I always provided dinner for my brother and myself. We ate a lot of peanut butter and jelly sandwiches. I loved going to school, because it got me out of the house. I liked learning, and I had a couple of really good friends there too. My good friends would come over my house and help me study, clean, make dinner, and help me take care of my eight-year-old brother. If my friends would help me, then it meant that I had more time to play.

When I was in high school, I was a cheerleader. I learned a lot about acrobatics from the other girls. It was very interesting, so I started taking classes to learn more. I took gymnastics and became very flexible, so by the time my junior year came around, I was the cheer captain. After high school, I planned to go to college but didn't go because I needed to stay home and take care of my mom and little brother. My mom got very ill, so I had to support the household.

My mom died from cancer a few years later. After she died, I stayed and I helped my brother until he graduated. My brother went off to college, and I moved in with a guy, and I lived with him until I died.

I died from a drug overdose. I took the wrong combination of drugs, which caused my heart to stop. I had bad chest pains while lying in bed, but they passed, then I fell back to sleep and did not wake. When I passed, I stood up and saw my body lying there in bed. I tried to cry but couldn't. I tried to wake my boyfriend but couldn't. I saw the light, and my mom was in the light. My mom told me, "Come with me," but I stayed behind to make sure everything would be okay without me. I followed my body to the hospital with my boyfriend. I followed my body everywhere until after I was buried. At the cemetery where I was buried, I met another spirit. She told me about her life and how to travel. As I saw the light, there was an angel that told me some simple rules if I was to stay on earth. One thing was to never move things in front of people, and only children under the age of five years old. We are not to scare people, and we can't become one with their body. We can't leave earth, and we can't fly. Also we can't kill people. I have been to every continent. I love Asia. The culture is so unique. I stayed in an old castle in Germany that no one else has been in a very long time. I like to go places that no humans can go to. I have been to the top of Mt. Everest. I went on safari with a group of people in Africa. I spent one year in India. Many spirits are in India. I stayed there long enough to learn their language. There was a lady there that could hear the spirits, and the spirits would line up to speak to her.

I like to travel and meet different spirits. There is a guy in South America. He stays with the Mayan pyramid. He is an ancient Mayan. Many spirits go there to speak with him. Most spirits don't go to the North Pole or South Pole because there are no people there, so there is no energy there. So if spirits totally run out of energy, then they must walk and not transport. I like to go to Antarctica and see the penguins.

All my feelings seemed to have carried over with me into my afterlife.

So if I were to give a message for all the living, it would be, travel and learn the other cultures while you are alive. They hold secrets that you must learn. Sarah was tired of all these travels. She had seen enough. She had heard about us from the other spirits that we were able to create the light, so she asked us to help her cross over. So we created the light, and Sarah walked into it, free from wandering the earth.

On May 12, 1996, I was thirty years old, and on this day, I died. I came from a family of ten children. I am the youngest. My name is Tammy Yates. My mother died when I was three. My older sisters pretty much raised me. I've taken ballet my whole life, since I was five years old. I didn't have very many friends because I spent all my time with school and practice. I performed ballet all over the United States. I performed in Ney York, Chicago, and LA a lot.

I grew up in LA. I was told that my mother loved the ballet, and I wanted to do something that my mother loved. I had one older sister who encouraged me and took me to all my practices. I practiced so much I missed out on my childhood. I stopped performing when I was twenty-six years old. I met up with an old friend from high school, and she showed me her party crowd. I went out every night with my friend. I learned how to drink and dance, and lots of boys. I partied, and the more I did, the harder we partied. My body wasn't used to everything. I used to take very good care of myself. I had been smoking crack cocaine. It became a little and then a little more. I ended up in the hospital from an overdose. My sister came and got me from the hospital. I stayed with my sister for a few months. I was trying to get my life back together. I didn't know what to do. All I ever knew was ballet. My sister kept telling me to get a job and figure out what I was doing with my life. She kept telling me to go back to school. I didn't want to go back to school, I wanted to find a good man, settle down, and have babies. I was out shopping one day, and I ran into my old friend that I partied with, so I went out with her that night. We partied hard. I thought it would be my one last time. I wound up in the hospital. I died in the ambulance from a crack cocaine overdose. I saw the light in the ambulance. I had no reason but to see what my sister had to say. My sister cried and said, "I tried to help you so much. Why couldn't you have listened?" When I travel, I visit my brothers and sisters. I travel to the old theaters where I had performed at. I visit lots of high schools. I follow the students around, wishing I was them.

I guess, if I could give a message to the living, I would say, know who you are and what you want to be for your whole life, and don't let others control you. What a tragedy this girl has gone through. Listening to an old friend, sometimes those old friends should just remain old friends. It was this friend that killed her, with her newfound drug addiction. We were able to create the light for Tammy. She went into it very quickly. She was so tired of traveling and doing nothing. She actually first approached us, asking if we could send her to the light. We told her yes, on one condition, that she would give us her story, and she did.

The day was June 1, 1962. I died at age forty-nine. My name is Ralph Zitterz. I was born in New York City, and my father owned a bakery. I had one brother, and we were Jewish. My brother and I were very close. We were only one year apart. My favorite season was winter. We would always play in the snow. In the winter, my dad would always bring home lots of warm rolls. My mother was a very good cook, so we ate a lot of good food.

When I was thirteen, I brought a girl home from school. My mom tried to feed her so much food that she didn't want to come back, but I convinced her that it was only because my mom liked her. So after I spoke with her, she kept coming back. Well, I ended up marrying this gal when I turned eighteen years old. I loved her hair. It was very long, very soft, and it was black. I was still married to her when I passed. I have two beautiful children, a boy and a girl.

My father had passed away, then I took over the bakery. I stayed in New York my whole life but had lung cancer from smoking. I had it for a couple of years before I died. The medical treatments were painful, so after one, I stopped going to them. I didn't smoke after I was diagnosed with cancer, because my wife was constantly yelling at me to stop smoking. I would continue to smoke secretly. One night, I was up all night because I couldn't breathe. I was putting my head into the ice chest to help me breathe. I passed out over the ice chest. I think I was alive for a few hours yet. My wife found my body the next morning. When she found me, I was standing next to her, looking at my body.

I did see the light and my aunt Sarah. She said, "Come with me, boy!" I asked her where she wanted me to go. She didn't say anything, so I turned back and saw my wife screaming. She called for the children and the neighbors, and she called her uncle at the mortuary, so he came and took my body. I stayed with my wife, who called everybody, and the house was full of people within one hour.

Then I stayed with my wife until it was her time to pass. Now I spend my time following my children. My daughter is fifty and still lives in New York. The boys are here in Ohio, and they have bakeries and are doing well.

I have traveled to places normal people can't get into. I have been to Israel, in the temples and synagogues.

If I were to leave a message, I would say, always listen to your wife, because she is usually right!Ralph had asked us to send him to the light, so Faith, my medium, made the light, and he walked into it.

I am always amazed when talking to these spirits, both young and old. The true stories we get from them, how they passed away, what they experienced from the time of their passing till now, things we all want to know, now are being revealed through speaking with these souls. Every bit of these stories is straight from speaking to these spirits. There is a chance you could know one of these spirits; maybe an old friend or a relative, you never know.

I always ask if there is a message they want to leave for us, the living. At most times, they do respond with a lesson learned in life and sometimes the afterlife also. It is very interesting to read their last message to the living. I have noticed it has a lot to do with the way their life turned out, maybe some missed information that they want to make sure you get.

Only thirteen, this next girl lost her life, as she will tell you in her own words. How exciting to her what happened by the soul themselves.

I'm Susan. I passed away when I was just thirteen years old. I was at a pool party. I was the oldest of three children. I remember my rocking horse. My mom still has it; it was my favorite toy. I played with it constantly. My mother tried to let my other siblings play with it once they reached the age, but I didn't like them playing with it, especially my brother.

I went to a private school (Catholic). I had lots of friends. If there was a party or gathering, I was invited. I had three close friends. We did everything together. We liked to go shopping, and we always had to have a mom with us. My mom hardly ever went because she worked and took care of all the other kids. My one friend's mom was a cosmetic consultant for Estée Lauder. She would put makeup on us and show us how to apply it. We always got free makeup. This is the same mom who had the pool party at her house. It was a very big house with a very large pool. We swam there all the time. I stayed the night whenever I could.

I was an excellent swimmer, but I didn't like the diving board. Everybody was doing odd dives, and they were all trying to outdo each other. I knew that I could do flips, so I tried to do a back flip, and it didn't work. So when I tried to do my back flip, I didn't flip far enough away from the diving board. So when I flipped, I hit my head and broke my neck. I died instantly. I saw myself floating on the water. I didn't know what to think. I kept yelling at myself for doing something so stupid. Two guys pulled me, my body, out of the water, then the ambulance arrived. I didn't know where to go. I just sat by the pool, staring at it. I saw an old lady in the light but didn't know her. I wanted to go find my mom first before I would go into the light. After a while, I walked home, and the light was still with me. I sat in my room on my rocking horse, waiting for my mom to walk in. I knew she would come in eventually once she found out that I was dead. She came in the next morning and lay on my bed, crying. When my little sister came into the room, she tried to sit on my rocking horse, but my mom yelled at her. I wish I could have told my little sister to go ahead and just ride it. I tried to speak to my mom, but she couldn't hear me. I stayed with my mom until after the funeral. I went home that night to go to my room, then I was going to go to the light after I said good-bye to my room, but then there was no light. So I went back to the pool where I passed away. There was a spirit there, which was my friend's dead grandmother. She told me, "Be careful of evil spirits, and listen to the angels' rules." She taught me how to travel, simply by closing my eyes and thinking about where I wanted to be.

I spent a lot of time in department stores when they were closed. I went to the art museum to stare at the pictures I wanted and to look at them as long as I wanted.

If I could leave a message for all the living, it would be, true friends are irreplaceable. Well, after missing the light when Susan first passed, she was able to go after my talk with her. Faith, my medium, created the light, where she saw the same little old lady that came for her the first time, who now came again to greet and welcome her home.

My next guest came to me late at night, in the middle of the night, and told me, "Man, have I got a story for you!" He went on to make sure that I was the one writing the book. He had traveled far to speak with me. After hearing all the spirits tell of me and how we can hear the spirits, he was so astonished; he had to tell his story. So I told him to come back that night, and I would take down his story, and it would be told.

I'm Jose Gonzales, and I died when I was twenty-five years old. I died on October 28, 2001. I had a brother. He was one year older than me. We lived with our dad most of the time, but sometimes with our grandma. We stayed with my grandma when my dad was out of town working. We liked staying with our grandma because she cooked very good food. We didn't like staying with her only because it was far from our friends' houses. When I was fourteen years old, my grandma died. It was very sad, and I still miss her. I always compared women to my grandma, and I couldn't find any that lived up to her standards.

I grew up in a rough area but never got involved with the crazy kids. My brother was involved in gangs, then he pulled me into the gang to make money, but of course, you had to kill someone that the gang didn't like to get into the gang. So one night, I killed someone that the gang didn't like. It was very hard, but after that, I was in, very close with everyone. After that, I started making a lot of money. I was selling weed and made very good money. I was about twenty-one years old when we started selling cocaine.

I moved into a very nice apartment in order to keep up with the clientele. I had to live close to my customers. I had a good lifestyle and lots of weapons. Security systems on cars, and my house, top of the line. I was saving my money so when I turned thirty years old, I could leave the country. I had a total of $3.5 million stashed away when I died.

My brother came to me one night. He was in trouble and needed $50K. I told him I had to go to the bank and get the money out. He got very mad at me and started tearing my place apart, looking for the money. I realized that he was very high. I tried to calm him down and told him that I would get him the money in the morning. He said, "You don't understand. I need the money right now!" He then pulled out his gun and started waving it around the room. I tried to grab the gun. We struggled for a while, destroying things. When the gun went off, it fired into the side of my neck. He started freaking out. He was screaming and crying profusely. I then grabbed him and pulled his ear close to my mouth. I told him that I was sorry that I didn't give him the money straight up. I told him how much I cared about him and how much he needs to get his life straightened out. I also told him to take all the money that I have, and I also told him how to pull the rest of the money out of the bank. I lay there. I couldn't breathe, and my brother was telling me how much he loved me and how sorry he was, then I died.

I saw my body lying there and my brother leaning over me, crying. I saw the light. I saw my grandmother. She was waving her hands toward me, but I stayed to make sure that my brother got all the money. My brother took all the money from inside the house and went and paid the people that he needed to pay. After that, my brother went back to his own house and packed himself some bags and sat in my car in front of the bank until it opened. My brother went into the bank and took the money out the way that I had told him to. He took a cashier's check for over $2 million.

I traveled to Mexico with my brother. I stayed there for a while, just watching him. Then I started wandering back toward the States. I didn't know what to do. Maybe I should find that light and go to my grandma. So I went back to Chicago and checked on a few friends and family.

Your energy field is known. Most of the spirits that I came across seem to have heard about it. I wanted to come see what it was about. When I arrived, a spirit was telling me about you and the stories that you are gathering, and they also told me that you would be able to send me to the light if I wanted to go. They also told me that you can hear the spirits talk, and we never have anybody that can hear us talk.

It was the conversation of the light that brought Jose to us. The spirits in the backyard near the energy field were telling him about us and how we can create the light, so Jose was very interested. So we made the light for him, and he walked on through.

My name is Diane Nostle. I was thirty-five when I passed away on February 12, 1971. I'm from Orlando, Florida. I miss my sister. She died at the age of three, and I was six years old.

I remember many years of crying. My mom blackened all the windows so the light wouldn't come in. My father left us about one year after my sister died. He still supported the family but couldn't live in the same house. I remember going to school. It was my sanctuary. I was never allowed to have friends come to my house. My mother would not allow it.

I had one very close friend. I would go to her house. There I would get to play, laugh, and eat candy. When it was time to go to high school, my friend was moving away. I had asked if I could go with my friend. I was not allowed to go, but I really wanted to. I did get to visit my friend in the summer when there was no school. The summer before my senior year of high school, I was with my friend for four weeks. While I was with my friend, I had met a guy and got pregnant. I didn't know I was pregnant until I got back to school. When I told my mom, she was excited that I was having a baby. My mother made me quit school until after I had the baby, then I went back to school and finished my senior year.

Every time I ate, I got sick, so I went to the doctor to see what was wrong. They ran test after test, and then I was diagnosed with stomach cancer. They put me through all kinds of treatments, chemo, and radiation. Then they told me I needed surgery to remove part of my stomach. I was very weak from the surgery, then one week later, I died.

I saw the light when I died. My mom and my little sister were in the light. My mom told me to come with her. I was unsure because I thought my mom was going to hell, and my sister was in heaven. It was also six years since I spoke to my mother. I didn't know that my mom had died. I wanted to go to the house to make sure that was my mom that I had seen. So after I died, I went to my mom's house. My father was there. I didn't expect him to be there because I didn't know the situation. My dad had moved back in with my mom to take care of her before she died. I stayed there for about one year, trying to get his attention. I would move his papers and things, hoping he would know it was me.

One day I left, and I was just walking around, so I wandered back to my old school, and then it was there I found other spirits. These spirits taught me how to travel. So I started going to different places. First, I traveled overseas to Italy because I always wanted to go there. I wandered all over Italy for a long time. My favorite place was Venice. There were lots of spirits there.

A spirit that I ran into in England told me about this energy field in the States. He said it was like a rush of energy for a spirit, so I had to come check it out. I was given an address of this place, so all I did was think about the address, and I was there. Once I was there, the other spirits showed me this energy field. I have been coming here for the past three years. About one month ago, I came by, and I heard that the owner of the house was talking to the spirits. The spirits also told me that you were writing our stories down, and if I wanted to tell my story, I could go in and speak with them. So I came in to talk with you.

Well, if I could leave a message for all the living, I would say, even if you don't agree with your loved ones, keep in touch, because you always want to know what happens to them. We sent this wonderful spirit to the light as she had asked us to do, where she'd seen her mother again in the light.

June 6, 1980, I was forty-seven years old. This was the day I died. My name is Rick Blanch. I had a basic childhood. I grew up in New York City. When I was twelve years old, my aunt came to live with us, my mom's sister. She came because her husband went to prison. I remember it being an exciting year with her coming to live with us, because she would buy us all kinds of toys, and she would take us out to the movies. My aunt paid a lot of attention to us, but she only stayed with us for a little over a year. My dad made her move. I was told she was causing trouble for our family.

I graduated from high school when I was seventeen years old, then I started working. I was in construction. I was an ironworker. I worked there for about ten years, then the company changed hands, then I had to find a new job. There was a nearby factory opening, so I took a job there. I was there for about three months, then my girlfriend told me she was pregnant with twins, so then we got married. Well, it wasn't quiet anymore at home. My wife stayed home and took care of the children. When the kids were about two years old, we moved into a nice apartment. I kept my job at the factory but also held a job as a maintenance guy at the building that I lived in. By having the maintenance job, it made things more affordable.

My kids had a virus that was going around in school. While we were vaccinated, my boy caught the virus. It was wintertime when the shots were being given out. I was sick, I had a cold. It made it easy for me to catch the virus. I was hospitalized for two months. I wasn't getting better. I got worse. My wife made me come home. She wanted me to pass at home. She was really fighting the doctors on this. When I came home, I was very glad to be home. I was home for three weeks before I died. I died in my bed, then my wife came in the evening and found me.

I saw the light. My mother was in it. I told her I wasn't coming yet. I wasn't coming home because I wanted to watch my kids graduate. I stayed at the house and watched my kids and my wife. She didn't stay at home too much because she was dating. I wanted her to be happy, but it felt really weird. Once she remarried, I left the house. I was hurt still; I still loved her. I would have liked to have gone to the light then but couldn't find it.

I was sitting in an office building, and another spirit came up to me and started talking to me and told me that I looked like I could use more energy. Then he told me about an energy field and told me he could take me to it, so we took off and hopped some cars until we got here, to this energy field. It was crazy filled with energy. I loved the energy, the way that it felt. So I went back to New York but come back here every so often. The last time I was here, I heard about you taking stories. Some creepy little girl told me to come in to give you my story and ask to be sent to the light.

My medium Faith created the light for this soul. He had longed to get back to the light that he had missed and to stop roaming the earth.

I'm Fred Turner. I died on February 19, 2002. I was sixty-two. I had been married for twenty-five years before my wife died. I had one son when my wife died. My son was twenty years old. My wife and I agreed to help our son to be the best that he could. Once my wife died, I was the only parent. My son was away at college when my wife passed. It was hard for me to call him home for that reason. My son spent one year at home after his mom died. It was a very hard time for both of us. I never remarried; it was too hard.

I died from emphysema, from smoking. I had been smoking since I was twelve years old. I collapsed at my home, then I called the neighbor lady. She then came over and called for an ambulance. They took me to the hospital and wanted to keep me there hooked up to machines, but I refused and came back home. That night, I couldn't breathe, then I passed away. The neighbor lady had stayed with me in the room that night. She was sleeping in my chair. When she woke up, she had seen my body and screamed because I was blue. She called for my son, and then she called the morgue.

When I was out of my body, I saw myself lying there, and I thought it was strange that I was seeing the room and everything in it. I didn't believe in anything after I died.

So I saw the light. It was a very bright yellow light, and I saw nobody in the light for me. I was very confused about what to do. I was confused because I was still standing in the same place that I passed away. Why didn't I move on? I stayed at my house for two weeks, then my son came home. I watched my son plan the funeral and clean out the house.

I travel back and forth from my son's house to the energy field in your backyard. I have been doing so for about eight years now. I travel back to my son's house in Alabama. I like to travel. I have been to San Francisco. I have sat at the top of the Golden Gate Bridge and then jump down.

If I could leave a message for all the living, it would be, believe the light is real, and don't just listen, but find out for yourself what is real! Believe, believe, believe! That's the message from all the spirits, it seems. So many souls have crossed over not believing in life after death. It seems that some think Jesus, heaven, and hell are all mythical places, but when they come to realize the truth, it is too late. So many wish to go back in time and listen to those who have warned them of all the things that are so important to take care of before we pass on. Unfortunately, I have spoken to so many that have avoided the light just because of fear of the unknown and uncertainty of their destiny. All this should have been taken care of in life, while they were alive. Once again, I must stress to you: these are *real* stories from those that have passed on. These stories are all from those earthbound spirits that roam the earth that missed or avoided the light.

October 10, 2009, I was in a bad car accident and passed away. My name is April Collins. I am from Cincinnati, Ohio. I was leaving a frat party with some friends. On our way home, there were three of us in the car, and I was the only one that passed away. I was coming from a frat party. I was the passenger, and I was thrown from the car. The other two girls that I was with lived. They both were very upset that they didn't die with me and was so sorry that I passed away.

My father was a doctor, and my mom stayed home and took care of my two sisters. I was raised in a family that gave me freedom to do whatever I wanted to do. I was a good girl but experimented with how far I could push my parents. When I was four years old, I stood in my room and screamed at the top of my lungs for a long time without punishment. One time, I turned on the water in the bathroom and left it on, just to see if I could get away with it. I was seven years old then.

When I got to high school, I liked to spend my mom's money. I was always at the mall. Me and my friends would try on clothes and put outfits together and pretend we were fashion models. I would buy things for my friends that couldn't afford things. When I was sixteen years old, my parents got me a new mustang for my birthday. After I got the car, I was almost never home. I was always over my girlfriend's house.

When I died, I saw my body lying on the ground. I kept yelling at my body to get up. I was scared. I wasn't sure what to believe. I did not believe that I was dead. I kept looking back and forth from the car to my body. I couldn't believe that I was dead. I went to my friends in the car and started yelling at them. I wanted them to go to my body and wake me up.

I saw the light, and I saw my grandmother in the light, telling me, "Come on!" I did not go because the light was annoying me. I followed my body to the morgue. I stayed with my body while my parents came to identify my body. My mom couldn't talk. She just cried. Dad was in disbelief that it was really me. I went to my funeral. A lot of people that I thought would come didn't come. From the funeral home, I went to the house of my friend who was in the accident with me. I tried talking to my friend. I yelled and screamed at her, but she couldn't hear me. From there, I started wandering around the mall. I realized that I could stay late after the mall had closed. Then I met another girl there that taught me how to travel and have fun as a spirit. We would rearrange things in the store at night.

Since I knew how to travel, we started going to different cities. The first city we went to was New York City. We had a blast there. We stayed there for like a month. We would rearrange stores at night. We visited places like the Statue of Liberty. We then visited all the big cities in the States. We went to Mexico, visiting spirits. Lots of evil spirits there. After Mexico, I went back home and kept watch over my parents and my sisters.

If I could leave a message for all those that live, it would be, when you think you have misplaced something, or something was moved, that you didn't move, it was probably a silly spirit like me. We created the light for this young, silly spirit. She once again saw her grandmother in the light, and she was able this time to go to her and was in heaven that night.

I'm Sam Willis. I died in June of 2002. I was in the hospital when I collapsed. Why? I don't know. I could hear some voices speaking to me while I lay there in bed. They were doctors, nurses, and family. I never left the hospital. I passed away in the hospital bed.

I'm from Ohio but grew up in West Virginia. I worked in construction. I was an electrician, among other things. I always preferred new construction over residential work. I was married when I was twenty years old. My wife and I had four children. One of the babies died at birth, so we had two boys and one girl still alive. My wife was never the same once the baby died. I raised my kids the best I could. So we didn't have everything, but we had enough. My wife died six months after I did. She never stopped crying since I died. When my wife passed, I was there. I saw her light and watched her go into it. I was happy that she went to the light, but I was very sad that I couldn't be with her. I still wish that I could be with her.

I saw the light and remembered all the hospital machines beeping and going off like crazy. My wife was screaming and crying in disbelief. She thought for sure that I would wake up, but I never woke up. I was standing right next to her, wishing I had woken up. She made the doctors try shocking me back to life for like a half hour, but I never came back to life. I went home with her that night while she cried. I was sitting on our bed. I never left her side until she died. I didn't think I had any place else better to be. After she died, I just wandered around and visited my kids. I never went very far.

I have been coming to your energy field in your yard for about four years. I want to leave a message for everyone reading this: please believe in Jesus Christ, and be nicer.Sam didn't want to go to the light because he knew he was going to hell. He told me how much he regretted not praying and believing that Jesus Christ was real. He thought that Jesus was just a well made-up story that sounded really good. He thought Jesus was a bunch of nonsense, but now he knows differently, and he tells all—believe!I'm Alice Davis. I'm from Tennessee. I died on September 1, 1988. I was thirty-two years old when I passed away.

I was born in the house we lived at, and I was the third child of eight children. My parents were farmers, so I had fun as a child. I got to play in the fields and climb trees. I liked to play down by the lake and skim rocks. I had lots of friends. We built from a rope that hung from a tree. We would swing over the water, then let go. We would fall into the deep end. One summer, one of my brothers jumped in and did not come back up. He died. My father then said no one else goes to the lake because of what happened.

Many years later, I went back to the lake with my daughter to swing over the lake again. The lake had become more shallow over the years, so I broke my neck when I jumped in. I was standing next to my daughter, trying to hold her, to comfort her. My daughter ran back to the house and got my mother. My mom ran down to the lake with my daughter, after she had called some neighbors for help. They dragged my body out of the water, then took me to the morgue.

I saw the light, and it stayed with me for several days. I had seen my aunt Elizabeth in the light. She said, "Come with me, pretty Alice." I stayed back because I thought that I could comfort my daughter. My daughter now talks to me. She asks me for help, but I can't help her.

I like to travel to the coast of Maine where the cliffs are. I also like the coast of England and Scotland. I have been to Australia. I love rocky coasts.

I want to leave a message for all the living: Go to the light when you die, because you can't help anyone here. No one can hear us. Alice decided to go to the light that she had once missed. She had been jumping off cliffs to try to reenact her death so she might get to see the light again but found out that it doesn't happen that way. We created the light for her, the light that she was chasing for so long that she wanted to get to.

I'm from Cleveland, Ohio, and I passed away on June 3, 1970. My name is Cindy Litera. I was raised by my grandmother and my aunt. I also had an older brother. I enjoyed band in school. I played the clarinet. I stayed home a lot, and I went to church a lot. I used to help my grandma cook dinner every night, and I always liked listening to my grandma's stories.

I moved away for a while after high school, for about one year. I went to Florida and stayed with my cousin. I waitressed and partied a lot. I met a guy while I was there, whom I dated for about three months, then he started hitting me. So I had enough of that, so I moved back home. When I moved home, I stayed with my aunt and grandma. Shortly after I moved back, my grandma passed away. I had a hard time with my grandma's death. I didn't know what I was going to do. So about six months after my grandma died, we cleared out all of her things. Then a friend of mine moved into the house with me and my aunt. My grandma had a substantial amount of money in her savings we didn't know about, like almost $100,000. I took some of the money and went to school to become a beautician. My life was pretty regular. I went to church and came home.

I had become very sick for about one month. I didn't know what was wrong, so I went to the hospital. They told me that I had a blood infection. They tried treating me, but I died. When I died, I saw the light, and my grandma was in it. The light followed me for about three days, and after my funeral, it disappeared. I didn't know where to go, so I would just walk around. One day, I was walking in a grocery store, and I bumped into someone I thought to be a person, but it was a spirit. It was a crazy old man, but he taught me a lot. He told me to just close my eyes and concentrate on where I wanted to be.

The first place I traveled to was London, England. I sat on top of a large bus and rode around the city for three days. After London, I went to Paris. I stayed in Paris for one week. Although I couldn't eat the food, I sat around, smelling it. I then went to Rome, Italy. I went and sat in the Vatican, and then I went to the Roman Ruins. From there, I went to the Great Pyramids in Egypt. Egypt is a scary place, with many evil spirits. Once I left Egypt, I then went back to my grandma's for a while to see my aunt. My best friend got married, and I got to sit up close where no one else could be. I enjoyed going places where no living person could go.

I want to leave a message for all the living: always have a strong belief, go to church, and always listen to Grandma!Cindy had asked Faith if she could send her to the light. She wanted to be with her grandma again. So Faith created the light, and Cindy once again saw her grandma in the light, waiting for her, so she went home after all the years of wandering around the earth as a traveling spirit.

May of 1942, I was twenty-two years old when I died. My name is Jackelyn Miler. I grew up in Detroit. I had one sister, and our father was a merchant. We had a little store where we sold a little bit of everything. My mom would sew cloths, then we would sell them at our store. I liked to go to the theater and watch movies, and I liked to go walking in the parks also.

High school was fun. I went to an all-girls school, a Catholic school. Once there was a stair well that only the teachers would use, so me and my girls got together and covered all the steps in glue. We didn't get punished for it, but another group of girls got blamed, and they had to clean up all the steps.

I was very sick for a couple of months. I was in bed and could not walk and had high fevers. Doctors would come to our house and give me medicine. My mom would stay with me most of the time. She would bring me cold towels and bathe me. One night, I was very delirious, and I could not see. I was reaching my hands out, trying to find my mom. I really didn't know where I was. That's all I remember, till I was standing over my body. My mom ran into the room, screaming, followed by my dad. They tried to shake me and wake me up. They called the doctor, then the doctor came and told them that I was dead. My mom, she cried for days.

I saw the light with angels, and I saw one of my aunts and my grandma in the light. They told me to come with them. I spoke with the angel, and he let me stay as long as I obeyed the rules, so I stayed. I stayed because I wanted to travel and see the world. I started walking. I walked down to the movie theater, and it was there that I met an old man spirit. He taught me how to travel, and he told me what to do.

The first place that I traveled to was California, because that's where they were making movies. I walked around the movie sets when no one was there. I was just admiring all that was there. After California, I went to Texas, but I didn't like it there, so I left quickly. I then went to London, England. I sat in a cathedral with no seats. I took a boat around in the river. I then visited a castle in Ireland. It was the one where you kiss the wall. I was looking for the Loch Ness Monster, but I didn't find him. Ireland has lots of parties, and they drink a lot. I also went to Egypt. I stayed inside the pyramids overnight, lots of evil in the pyramids. There was talk amongst the camps how people became lost and never came back from inside the pyramids. I think that place is very secretive, and it holds many secrets.

I would like to leave a message for all the living: reality is definitely not what it seems! Jackelyn went to the light that night, after wandering around for seventy years. She knew this was the year of 2012 and was longing to get to the light to see her grandma and aunt again. Traveling the earth compared to heaven…there is none.

I have been speaking to so many spirits over the last few months, and it seems a lot of them miss the light to continue checking on family that lives. I think that so many are confused at the time of death, when they see the light, thinking that they can actually help the living family, which is not true. The spirits can only observe what goes on here in the living world.

I have heard, while writing this book, about Bible beliefs. Some say that the Bible does not support anything about the light. After speaking with over seventy spirits and hearing the similar stories about the light and what happens at that given time, I have a very strong belief about what will happen when you pass. Most Christians are taught that once you die, you will go to heaven or hell, and this is true, to a point. I was taught the same belief. I was raised a strong Baptist, but I have a different take on things now. I now know that once you die, you will meet an angel at the time of your passing, and it is at this time that you will be given a choice to make. The angel will give you an option to stay on earth as an earthbound spirit or to move on into the light where you will face your eternity. If you choose to stay, you will be given five specific rules that you *must* follow. I spoke of these rules while I was speaking to the spirits. If you do not obey these rules, you will be chained and pulled into the light, without a choice. Once you see the light, it is then you will either have someone waiting in the light for you, or nobody will be there. If nobody is seen in your light, this means you will probably end up in hell. So when you pass through this light, there will be two demons waiting on your soul to take you to hell. Now if you see someone in your light to greet you, then you will also be greeted by angels that will welcome you into heaven. You would probably see some old friends or family members that have passed on and went to heaven in your light at the time of passing.

Now there are some souls that have sinned so badly and committed awful sins. These souls are gathered by four demons at their time of death. When these souls pass on, there are the four demons that will chain these souls and drag them kicking and screaming straight into hell.

It is these souls that are taken off to their light and dragged straight to hell. They have no choice to stay on earth or go to the light. It is because of their sins that God has judged them accordingly—some of the seven most deadly sins and for the sins of man hurting the innocent children. God has always looked after the small children, with all their innocence. God still has judgment day coming. It is at this time that all the spirits on earth will be judged. They will have no choice. They will all face God and their eternity.

For those that missed the light or decided to stay, they knew about judgment day and what they would face. We all need to remember in the Gospel of John 14:6. This is where Jesus tells us that He is the way, the truth and the light and that no man comes unto the Father but by Him. You see, it is Jesus whom we must pass through to get to heaven or hell. It is He who is the light we see when we pass, and it is in Him what matters, how we believe in Him, that will decide our destination.

I was sleeping one night, when I was awakened by a spirit. This was a very strange thing that happened that night. I was sleeping, when suddenly I was having visions of Michael Jackson singing and dancing in my thoughts. It was then that I heard a voice telling me that he had a very important story for me to write. It was Michael Jackson that came to me with a very important story and a very-much-needed message for all his children that he gave me. It was Lucifer that had brought him straight up from hell to speak with me. So within the next two days, I would speak to Michael Jackson.

It was in my house where Lucifer brought Michael Jackson in chains, hand to foot, accompanied by a demon, who could not leave Michael's side. My medium Faith could not hear the spirit of Michael Jackson because of the demon that was with him. So Lucifer would tell Faith what Michael was saying, then she would tell me. This was very strange to me, to have the Michael Jackson here wanting to speak to me. Lucifer told Michael that I was writing a book and asked Michael if he had a story and a message he wanted to tell his children. So the following story is true and is straight from Michael Jackson as he has told me to write it. There are things that he told me that only family and very close people will know. I told Michael that I need to know things that no one else would know to prove to everybody that I was not making this up, but that I was indeed speaking to the king of pop.

The day that I spoke to Michael Jackson was April 17, 2012, and this is what he had to say:I wanted to die. I was done with the world. I was suffering. I was in a lot of pain. My doctor listened to me for a great deal of money. I had said good-bye to my family before I died. My family knew that I planned my death, and no one was to know this. My family does not know this, but there is unfound money. If they go through my paperwork, they will find it. There is property in the Cayman Islands that I own. The key to find the money is on my property, a small piece of property.

I planned my death for two months. My family only knew for one week. Some of my family tried to talk me out of it, the girls, my sisters. They didn't understand the suffering. It was a good way to go out, for my fans to think I was killed or, more mistakenly, overdosed. The doctor wanted the money for his family as well. I gave him different amounts. I gave him $2.2 million dollars for that incident. I also gave him cash here and there. I couldn't even tell you the amounts. I committed suicide, which took me straight to hell, among all my other sins. I must tell you that money does not buy you happiness, because even your family turns against you.

I have a message to my children. This is something in addition to the letters that I left you before I died.

To my only loves,

Believe in Jesus Christ. Do not lose your way. Do not listen to others. Trust no one but each other. Do not let the money ruin you. Do not live in vain, and the pictures that I gave you, continue to kiss them.

Believe these words as they are true. Remember what I sang to you,

"Pink Elephants."

This completes the message.

At the time of my dying, I did see the light and walk into the light. I had thought that I was going to heaven, but when I went through, I was met by four demons. They chained me up and took me to hell. The demons told me why I was going to hell. It was because I didn't ask for forgiveness for my sins. I had told my family that I would see them again in heaven.

I had faith as a child, but my faith weakened as an adult. We did go to church, but when we came home, we did all the same sins again. I know that I was blessed with many talents, singing and dancing and other things, so I thought because I was blessed that I would go to heaven.

My torture is having a demon attached to me throughout eternity that reminds me that I knew of Christ but did not believe, and that is why I am in hell.

I want to tell my family, I am so sorry I will not see everyone in heaven, and I hope that I will not see you in hell. The song "This Is It" was a song for my fans, with a message. I needed to tell them some last things after I passed. A day or so after my passing, I did go back to Neverland Ranch to see it a last time. All the fame in the world and all the money in the world could not get me to heaven. I missed the opportunity I had on earth. "This Is It" is about seizing opportunity when it is right in front of you. I have had time to think and look back upon my life. My life had one direction, and I lived it. Oh god, I wish I could go back and change things. I know that I hurt my family and especially my mother. My children are my loves and forever will be. I want to make sure that the message I gave to them will reach them. It is important. My life was an open book for all to see. Some chapters were very dark.

There are other messages I left for my fans. They just need to listen to a few of my last recordings. I had to leave something, so I decided to leave it as the Beatles would by backmasking in their years, a message for all to hear played backwards. These were some of the things that I learned from Paul.

I want to tell my sisters, you were right! They will understand.

While speaking to the spirit of Michael Jackson and hearing his story, it makes me stop and think. To have a head of knowledge and to believe in your heart are really two different things. You see, Michael tells us that he knew of Christ and even went to church but never asked for forgiveness of his sins. He also lost his faith along the way.

It was Lucifer that brought me the spirit of Michael Jackson. Lucifer knew that I was writing this book and Michael had a message for his children and family and knew that through this book, all could be reached.

I have been talking to Lucifer throughout this book. I have sat with him and interviewed him in my house. Upcoming are true stories from Lucifer as he only can tell them. Things in the world that have happened and things to come—these are only a few of the things that Lucifer will speak of. Know that Lucifer is very much real, and remember that it was only Lucifer and God before man was created.

The sons of man, or the Greek gods as you might know them, these are the twelve fallen angels, which I will also speak with. We will talk of their jobs on earth, like controlling the four elements (earth, wind, water, fire). You will see that each god is different, and they all have their own way, but all work together. But first, I will speak to Lucifer and let him tell us a few things that we didn't know. Now read as Lucifer tells us some things we didn't know.

God would tell me everything. He told me how He created me, and He told me how He created the universe. He told me how He created everything on Earth. I was the only one allowed in

His chamber. He would give me things to create, and I would create them. I created the serpent and all the things that bite. God questioned my creations, because He thought that I was trying to create something more powerful than His creations. He would create a bunny, then I would create a snake to eat it. He created the lamb, and I created the lion. When God created man, I couldn't create any higher.

He went to earth as a trial to test man, and man passed. He came back, and then I got to go test man. Man did not pass my test, so God was angry. He had created something both good and evil. We fought a lot, and then He no longer told me anything. He wanted me to go. There was a five-thousand-year gap between creation and the creation of man.

I was thrown out of heaven and cursed to my belly. I had to learn and fight to get back to my form. I did not hear from God for a long time. I learned to take on my new forms step by step. Every time I found myself in a new form, I discovered more powers. I could move mountains like God, and water, and eventually I found out I could move everything. This time it angered God.

I moved the tree of life. I moved it from one country to a place you can't find it. This is present day, and the tree is still where I placed it. After I moved the tree, God pulled me back into heaven. He told me enough and that I was done having my fun. He thought He was going to keep me in heaven, but I told Him that I was going back. He said, "Not like that." Then He told me I was staying. We battled for many years. I did get to go back and control the earth until the end of time. There was a sect of angels that I was in control of. They took my side when I was fighting with God. God pushed them away, so they went down to earth on their own. They wreaked havoc with the humans. We were not paying attention. They became gods amongst the humans. They taught them our secrets. They taught them how to move things without touching them. They were trying to give the humans powers to be like gods. By mating with them, their offspring would be very powerful. God could not touch them like he could the angels. God could not touch the offspring. He would not condemn them for their powers.

There was a time when God said enough of the angels doing what they wanted to do, so God took back control. It was at this time when the Great Pyramids were built in Egypt and Mexico. The humans used their angelic powers to move rock.

When we were done fighting in heaven, I told God that I would go and I would control the sons of man and all the angels that have gone from heaven. They would all be in my control. God made the deal with me, that I could keep thirteen sons of man and also I would get to keep five hundred angels that left heaven to be in my control. This became our separation. There was no more fighting between Him and I.

Jesus came to my land. He knew the spot where the evil was. Jesus knew that I would come. He sat under an olive tree, waiting for me. My first question to Jesus was, "Why do you suffer for Him?" "Why do you humble yourself to these people?" "You could wave your hand and destroy them all." "I want you to leave this place. Over there"—as I pointed to the land—"is the food you need and the wine you drink. A few steps and it's yours." The food was there waiting. I would point to the food and tell Him to get it.

I could not touch Him. I would circle Him in the air, telling Him that He was no better than the humans. I told Him that He was not a God, but that I was more of a god than Him. I would spit on Him, and I tempted Him with things that were mine and His. He cried to God and got no help. He was weak. I almost had Him. There was no hope. He was going to stay His way. I left the food, and I left also.

I take men before God every day and beg for their souls. This is like a game, a stopping and starting point.

I have control of many nations when there is a ruler I can control. I had control of George W. Bush, Richard Nixon, Abraham Lincoln. I also controlled the Kennedys. I destroyed John F. Kennedy Jr., because he was not in my control. He would have been his own person. I have many nations in my control. I have China, Japan, Korea, Vietnam, India, and South Africa—all in my control. They move drugs, money, gold, diamonds, and other precious gems. I control all of South Africa.

Lucifer was present during the planning of 9/11. Lucifer will now tell us the truth of 9/11, the true target, and the way it all went down. This is something our governments do not want us to know.

There was a meeting. I was there. Military people were planning to take him out. He was very powerful. He was from Japan, and he was trying to bring weapons to the five nations that destroyed him. All the military officials came to the conclusion that he had to die. He was almost untouchable, but on the day of the attack, he would be at the pentagon. If it was a terrorist, no one would think anything else. The whole world knew the Middle East was after the United States. We had to make the focus big, make it seem like the main goal was the Twin Towers. The Pentagon was the main goal. So a plane and a missile was fired into the Pentagon. The missile hit the Pentagon first, then the plane, and then the United States government covered it up.

Russia wanted this guy taken out, so they told us to do whatever was necessary.

There was a circle of five governments involved. They were the United States, Libya, China, Arab, and Cuba. These all help plan the attack on the Twin Towers 9/11. There were to be five planes involved in this attack. The fifth plane never left Washington DC's airport. The plane that left LaGuardia's airport had a destination to go to Philadelphia.

This guy was trying to move weapons of mass destruction to different countries, so Russia gave orders to take this person out because of competition. From all of this, I get control of all countries involved, and I get to make future decisions.

Obama is in office for a reason. He is moving troops out of the Middle East. He will continue to fight to get them out. He has to prepare the land for what is coming. They must fight amongst themselves. Starting at the end of his earth's cycle, all the descendants of Him and them must die. It is God's will, to kill off the descendants of men. The goal is for the United States to be completely out of the Middle East. Obama will get this done.

George Washington's father was the first Free Mason, a secret society made to hold the secrets of most powerful men, secrets of development and technology. The Free Masons would control when something could be released (new technology). They started out as a Christian group. They kept too many secrets, and evil found its way in, as it always does.

They have many hidden places, old places, places that no one would ever think to look, under the mansion where the Underground Railroad starts and Thomas Jefferson's mansion. I appeared to Thomas Jefferson once. I had drinks with him in a bar. He did not know who I was. He was much more shy than you think. He kept their secrets very well.

There is an old church still standing and still has its bell. It is in Baltimore, Maryland. The sign on the church is "The First Baptist Church." This is the second secret place of the Free Masons. There is a carving inside the church that depicts the human's picture of the devil.

The Roman Catholic Church controls a lot of people. They brainwash you. They can teach you how to worship false idols and control your mind. Catholics have been around forever.

The Vatican holds many secrets. They control ancient documents, and they tell everyone how to interpret these documents. They are expert liars.

One old secret is that the church knows about the gods, the sons of man. They have documents to prove them real. These documents were written in 3000 BC. There are stories of how the pyramids were made and how the gods control the earth. This document is kept in a vault way down inside the Vatican. No one has looked at them in over one thousand years because of too much technology today. They have been locked down.

The church controls banks; they own many banks. Money laundering, they move money all throughout Europe. This is a new thing that they have been doing for the past two hundred years. No one expects the church. These are the days that you will find the Vatican locked down, because they move drugs and money. It is a clean import-export business.

The new pope changed things to put them back to the old way. He is doing this to confuse the people of the church. It will drive some of them away. It is the starting of the breaking up of the church.

The Antichrist is alive. He will come out of the land of the Israelites. He will appear within a decade [ten years]. He is well protected. His family is very prominent. He has been chosen but does not know it yet. He will know within the next three years. He has the powers in him already. I have prepared his mind already. He will be strong. He will take his seat at the United Nations, then he will have mind control over all the weak. Everyone will receive a mark, the mark of the beast [Lucifer]. The years march with the stars.

Rock stars are inspired by me. Bret Michaels gave me his hair for fame and glory. The Rolling Stones, they wanted years of fame, which I gave them, but some of those years were bad years, so in the bad years, I collected from them, like a roller coaster.

Elvis gave up his life for good songs. He would torture himself. He could not make up his mind between his family and the road.

Led Zeppelin's Jimmy Page called upon me first. He could not believe that he could have everything that he asked for. He asked for the ultimate package—fame, fortune, and all that goes along with it. The bandmates also made a deal with me. With Robert Plant, I took his son, and Bonham gave me his life within years. So Jimmy Page made the deal that cost his bandmates. Jimmy Page brought me the rest of the band, so he did not owe me anything.

The way we spoke to Lucifer was amazing. We would call for him to come and speak with us regarding things that only he would know. He would come right through my medium Faith. Her voice would change, and her countenance would also change. It really wasn't too scary as one might think. He has been known to appear to people in the flesh. He can take on the image of a man, a man you would never know or suspect, one that might be eating dinner right across from you. My medium was also a witch. She had belonged to a coven when she was younger, and she did meet Lucifer then, as a man and also in his true form. So because I was writing this book and we were talking to the spirits also, we thought that we would ask Lucifer to be a guest in my house and to speak of things from the very beginning of time and also what is going on in today's world. So we would speak with Lucifer for a total of four days and like two hours a night. During the time of speaking to him, he would come to the house often.

I grew up in church and went to a Christian school, so I was well educated in the Bible. I knew of Lucifer, God, and the sons of man. Since we were talking to Lucifer already, I thought, why not see if we can speak with the twelve fallen angels, or the sons of man? I thought this would make good reading, because no one else has ever spoken to all twelve gods before. I asked Lucifer if we could maybe get a chance to do so, so he arranged that we would speak to a god per week. Talking to all the gods took time, like a couple of months. These fallen angels, you might also know them as the Greek gods and the gods of the elements. Four of the gods control the four elements—fire, wind, water, and earth. As you read with our conversation with Lucifer, you can see how many things were spoke about that not even the Bible tells us. All this information answers some questions from the beginning of time.

We all know that Lucifer is evil, but after speaking to him throughout the writing of this book, he tells me he carries out God's will. He has respect for God, as he appears before Him each day. I would ask Lucifer a question, and his response would be, "If it is His will." You see, Lucifer is only as evil as God lets him be. The relationship that Lucifer and God had in the beginning was amazing. God had taught Lucifer how to create. Then as we know it, he gets asked to leave heaven, but still Lucifer is the only one that is allowed to go back and forth between heaven and earth. While the other twelve that left heaven are not allowed to leave earth, and they must answer to Lucifer, they are his responsibility. So now we will talk to the Greek gods, or the sons of man, as they are known. Each one of these gods sat with me and my medium Faith, and they told their story as only they can tell it.

I am William. I was created after Noah and before Christ. I hang around the places of the sea. I can only do what God allows me to do. He fights with me on the winds of destruction. When He wins, He is happy. I bring the storms of the sea, hurricanes, tsunami, and tropical storms also. I live in what you call the Bermuda Triangle. I am the demon which caused all the disappearances of ships, planes, people, and boats in the triangle. I will take more souls this year than the previous one hundred years. Your waters are changing. The triangle will also change. Boats and planes will misread numbers of where I am located. Watch for signs. The stars that are above me will change. Do not take a ship that way.

I was one of the sons of man. I am Poseidon, the water god. I am god over all waters. It was the fallen angels, or the sons of man, that help build the ancient pyramids in Egypt and Mexico and all stone structures. We used our angelic powers to move the rock to create the pyramids, and we gave technology to the people.

I can possess men, as truly I am one of the sons of man, and water god.

All Egypt, Greek, Roman, and European gods are all one and the same. All were the fallen angels.

I am Hephaestus, the god of fire. The first time that I came down to earth from heaven, I was unsure of what I would be doing. I got to choose fire. I was not a very pretty angel. The Greeks saw my deformity, but I could hide in the fire. Since I took fire, I was in control of the molten earth. I could erupt volcanoes, and I could fill the seas with hot lava and make land. My competition was the sun, because the sun can also bring fire. I also can bring fire from the lightning.

I have taught man how to use fire to forge metals. I enjoy doing this. I enjoy being in the shops [metal]. I enjoy watching men make things using my fire. Often I didn't use any firepower for a while, but when they let me, I can get to erupt volcanoes and change earth. I helped men make their tools to build the pyramids. Their tools were made of gold.

I was not as good looking as most of the gods. I raped many women when I was in the physical form as a man. I had many children. I do not know the number of children. I still crave the flesh of a body. I am one of the few that can possess.

Yellowstone National Park has volcanoes, and it will be this eruption that will end the earth as you know it. It will take out the whole Northern Hemisphere in a matter of a few days. It is ready to go any day. The heat has risen as high as it can without blowing.

The Catholics are using the circle book of spells to time-travel and figure out the future, but they don't know what they are doing. No one of the ancient wisdom has helped them, because no one has asked for help.

Artemis is the goddess of earth, and now she will tell us why she chose earth and her duties to earth.

I was drawn to the trees. I wanted to care for the trees and everything in the trees. The forests are my favorite place to be. I am upset that humans are destroying them. The earth cycles are changing; stars and planets are moving. Things will be different in drastic measures. Do not expect our weather to be as expected. The earth is moving in a new direction. It is fun for me to make these changes, but sad for you. Many people will die during these changes, and a lot more natural disasters as you call them.

Your rainforest will not all be destroyed, but there are humans still destroying it.

As goddess of the earth, I control all that grows. I control the animals of the forest, and I control earthquakes. When people pray to me, I will answer those who believe that I exist. I have always helped, if I can, the ones who see me when they touch me. When Jesus died, we were no longer allowed to appear before men.

The leader of all the gods, or sons of man, is Zeus. He is the one in full control of all the gods; he answers to Lucifer. If the other gods get out of line, then Zeus will tell Lucifer, then he steps in and deals with the god or gods that are out of line. It is in this chain of command that God wills it. Zeus is very interesting, because he is over the weather and works with a lot of the gods.

I got to choose first. I wanted to control the skies. Since I got to choose first, I wanted to control the most powerful element. Choosing this at the time, I didn't know but put me in control of the rest of the gods. I enjoy being in control. This sometimes makes the other gods mad at me. We have many fights, and if they don't like what I say, they can go away. My actual powers are equal to the other gods, but I have powers that they don't have.

We helped build the pyramids and many ancient cities. I make the storms, lighting, and thunder. They are all mine. I work with Poseidon and Artemis. She is tricky to work with. Poseidon and I created the flood for God. I enjoy working with Poseidon.

My favorite thing to do is to make love to all the women that I am allowed to. I control all the winds and rain.

The ancient people listened to us, the gods, as we picked our names, and those are the names that we like the most, because we were allowed to help choose them.

Aphrodite, the goddess of love, is an interesting goddess, a very caring over-the-top goddess. She will tell us a little about love and who she has been helping by making them beautiful.

By choosing this [love], I was able to possess more. I am displeased that I am not allowed to do this as often now as I could back in the beginning. Look to the beautiful, powerful women of ancient times, because it's a man's world now. Cleopatra was mine. Hera, the wives of all the Pharaohs, Josephine, Napoleon's wife, Marie Antoinette, Catherine the Great, and Helen of Troy—all of these were women that I helped stay beautiful and in love. I helped the beautiful women become powerful. The next queen of England is mine.

Roses, cherry blossoms, tiger lilies, and the black walnut tree—these are all under my control. Real lace from the silkworm, anything in painting that is beautiful, or other arts, a lot of Monet's are mine. Michelangelo, I helped him and guided him through the painting of the Sistine Chapel. I would work with any architect that would ask me for my help to design beauti-

ful buildings or cars and carvings. I worked with
many Indian cultures a lot. I work with Martha
Stewart. It is hard now these days to make people
fall in love. There has to be a chemistry. People
rush too much at a very fast pace. Love is not
what it was or meant to be. Take your time and
find your love is what I would tell people today.
Never hesitate to make the world more beautiful
if you can.

Athena, the goddess of war, is a very powerful goddess, one that
loves control, starting wars all over the world and controlling them.
Every war that was and is going on now, this goddess controls. She
is a very beautiful woman, but very dangerous too. Her beauty will
distract you while she kills you. It is she who is also a sex demon, as
is most of the goddesses. These are also called succubus. They love to
possess women and have sex with the women's husband or boyfriend,
and oftentimes the guy doesn't even notice. Aphrodite is also another
one that will possess. Not too many people pay attention to this. It
usually will go on unnoticed. You see, all the gods had bodies of flesh
when they came to earth the first time and mingled with all those on
earth. It was then that they would have children that were godlike,
because the children were half angel and half of earth. These children
would possess great powers and learn all the ancient spells that were
brought from heaven. So this is why the goddess more than the gods
love to possess man. They crave the flesh for sex and satisfaction, and
once you give in and they know that you know who they are, then it
will become a habit or a necessity for them to possess to please their
desires. This, of course, is done throughout the world. Many men
have had sex with these goddess and have not even known.

I wanted to have as much control as I could, so
that is why I chose to be the god of war and of
art. I chose to be a woman, and my God-given
name is Darna, but I also like Athena. My spe-
cialties in craft are weaving, pottery, which is my
favorite, and also the art of buildings. I ride a
horse with wings [Pegasus]. I can make people of

a nation fight. I control the fighting and can stop it as well.

George Bush caused all the wars during his time in office. George Bush likes wars. He thinks that they are manly. He doesn't think that we should have a military if they are not fighting. He tries to be like Mussolini and other great leaders of war. Bush was chasing Bin Laden to create more wars. These are men who want to be famous at a great price.

I like wars that stay inside their own countries. The best warriors were the Native American Indians. They were the fewest people to fight for true reasons when they fought. It was not political. The fun wars are the religious wars; it brings out the strongest people. The Roman Crusades were fun. The Crusades came across as a highly religious war but was not. It was about gathering land.

I also worked with God, with the Israelites in their battles of Old Testament times. I was also involved in the dynasties. These wars were with Genghis Khan. He was fighting for the land. I put my blessing of war upon him.

The harshest wars are done by using strategic moves, and no weapons, only a mind and a pen. Men that get together and discuss how to hurt people without hurting people, a cheap war. Hitler was looking to take over the people and not the land. Hitler was brilliant. He planned everything and didn't go into it blindly. He made himself a personal army, like the old cardinals of France. He spent a lot of his time by himself. Hitler was an individual planner. He knew what he wanted, and he didn't want anyone else to interfere. His plan worked for him.

People want to have a group of people all agreeing together, so if a war was to be started, then the group is in place already. God is always with Israel, and they will win their wars.

I am the god of the dark wars. I help rule the wars between the gods. I chose to be this god myself. I must keep them from killing each other. They must work together at all times, but they don't always. If a fight breaks out, I step in. I am the god who knows where all the other gods are. Lucifer can't kill any of the other gods. I was appointed by God Almighty in heaven before the fall of the angels, to direct and make sure there was no fighting. I watch over the other five hundreds angels as well.

The last time that I possessed someone was two days ago. The man was sleeping, so I entered the man's body. I stayed about two hours. I fucked his wife for about two hours. I can possess people to make them kill people or themselves. Cats protect the underworld.

There is a male group of warlocks. They are in London. A couple of them can hear me. They think that they are worshiping me, but I can't answer prayers or do anything that they request. They must pray to God or Lucifer. They are a unique bunch. The Greeks worshiped us very well. There was one follower that presented us to council, so their land became our land. We all appeared to the Greeks in physical form. We each showed them what we could do, to make them believe. We made them write down everything in their doctrine, their official guides. They didn't believe in the one true God, but they believed in us because they could see us. They have statues and temples that still stand to this day, for worshiping us, and still today worship us.

It was about nine thousand years ago that we came down to earth, before the Great Flood. It was then that we could still go back and forth between heaven and earth. There are only a few that hear the spirits, even fewer that hear that also believe.

Hera is the god of marriage and magic. She has a unique job, and she too is also a succubus, who loves and craves sex from humans.

> I protect families and marriage and magic. I also protect things for the gods. I can possess also. My main focus is keeping people married and relationships together. I married Zeus seven thousand years ago. I hardly see him because he is very busy. My magic is to protect things, so if I place a spell on something, it becomes invisible to the naked eyes. You will never find these things. I protect things for governments, only if Lucifer will ask me, like for the US. There are books in the library of Congress. I protect weapons of mass destruction for other countries, so the other countries and their scouts will not see the weapons. The things in the sea I also protect. I work with Poseidon.

The sun god was very popular with the Egyptians and other ancient cultures. In Egypt, he was known as Ra and worshiped throughout the land. It was because without the sun, there was no life. So they worshiped him. The Greeks called him Apollo, a very powerful god and one of the fallen angels. As I spoke with Apollo, he was a very nice god, easy to speak with, and polite. He answered all my questions and even gave some information to us that we didn't know.

> I chose the sun because it is a powerful force. I like the brightness of the light. I hate being in the dark. I knew that God prized the sun. That is why I am the sun god. I have been called the sun god but do not see myself as the god of the sun, but I still exalt God, even though I still have powers to work with the sun.

The sun is changing as the earth is changing. It is necessary to complete the cycle. The earth's temperatures will change. You will get warmer but not as fast as some of your scientists say. The sun is not causing all of the changes. It is the earth and the sun together. It is God's wishes for the changes. I do not do anything to the sun that God does not wish. The solar flares are almost like earthquakes to the sun. They change the behavior of the sun. Nothing you will notice just yet, but it will come. Your days and times will be changing shortly. You will notice it more and more over the next few years. Most people will not pay attention to the changes in the day and night, but if you pay attention, you will see them.

Egyptians were obsessed with the sun. All the cultures were obsessed with the sun, because it was their life. They thought that life would not exist without it. The Egyptians were overobsessed. They would not do anything without consulting me first. They would go as far as to bury people only when the sun was in a certain part of the sky. If a birth came at night, the child would be considered evil and not born into the light. I helped with the construction of the Great Pyramids. I helped the alignment of the pyramids with the sun. They were aligned to keep track of time, to be in line with the sun, moon, and stars. Egyptians would do things according to the time of day, the way the sun appeared in the sky. Mayans were not as picky but more savage. The Mayans had it correct, the sun and their calendar days; they figured it out themselves without help from the gods.

The governments are blaming these toxic gases for global warming. It is bad to breathe, but it is not causing the global warming. The sun is making its cycle. It must be heated, as the earth is making its cycle also. They work together. Scientists say the inside of the earth is heating, just as much as the outside. They tell people about the inside, but the government doesn't care, because they can't see it. If the governments would step aside and let the scientists talk to the people, the people would understand and not blame it on the sun. People need the sun more than they think, but the destruction will come from the earth and sun. This combination will eventually destroy the earth.

Do not blame the sun, but blame yourselves for the earth's destruction. The worst you are, the faster the destruction will come! Talking to Apollo brought some light in on some questions about the global warming and the weather changes that we are going through. I think that just about all the gods were warning us about the changes in the weather and how it is changing drastically. We can just look out our windows and see all the differences. It seems cold when it should be warm, and warm when it should be cold. I know this. The year of 2012, our spring came very early. I'd seen the trees having leaves before April 1. This March was a very warm one, and April was cold. A little crazy, it seems that they traded spots. I know a lot of people are looking to the Mayan calendar to see what will happen to us, because as Apollo said, it seems like they had their calendar correct.

The god of homes and hearth is Hestia. She would make sure that the home was comfortable and warm. Back in time, the hearth was everything. It is where the family would get warm and where the food was prepared, so it was a very important place in the home. She would see to it that the hearth was taken care of. Now we will see why Hestia chose to be the god of home and hearth.

I chose this because I like being at home and very comfortable, and there really wasn't much left for me to choose from. I make sure that the houses are taken care of, and I remind people to keep up on their houses, to keep up on repairs, and also if there is trouble in the home, I can call other gods or fairies to help.

I make sure that the hearth is working, and if it is broke, I let the homeowners know, if they ask me. I have helped the Egyptians by taking care of the stones around the fire. I made sure that they had food in their homes and enough people to help run their house. If there was an area lacking, I would help with it. I am helping people restore their homes from war. These are small wars, wars where people destroy each other's homes, like Russia and in that area.

Being a god is very nice because we get to know everything. If we don't know something, we can find out. We can go and read people's minds, and we get to talk to each other and learn about things we don't know about from the other gods. I get to learn when disasters will happen, and Aphrodite will tell us about the latest loves. Gods are special because they were angels once but then fell from heaven. The Greeks took to us and gave us our names as you know us.

Hermes is the god of business, and I had a chance to sit with him and talk. Here is what he had to say.

My God-given name is Alterne.

I chose business because I thought that it would be easy. I didn't want to leave heaven, but I followed my love, Aphrodite. I do miss the peacefulness of heaven, and I didn't have to do anything there. I work with corporations and their board of directors. I teach them strategies for business, teaching them what they need the most, how to make money using their own money. I bring in people that know business, that can show them what to do. I did work with Sony. I showed them how to expand. I brought them a very good marketing person.

I'm also known for thievery, stealing. Once is noted. I stole the fire from the arena. I put it in the sea for a while. Some things that I stole and got away with like cars and things from the gods, it was fun for a minute. Once, I stole a star. I called it to me, but I had to put it back quickly because God came after me. I had moved but didn't steal important documents for a moment.

When starting a new business, don't be foolish about your money and your staff. Don't let your business be run by other people. Watch it! You must always be selling and marketing as a business. You always need to do this, or there is no business. Take others' opinions, but not their advice. This is the best advice to give.

We now have spoken to eleven of the twelve gods, or fallen angels. All their jobs and what they can do—all are very interesting. We know that all have a few things in common. I believe that they all wish that they had never left heaven. All the gods still exalt God Almighty, and all do his will. When a storm is coming, it would be Zeus controlling the wind and thunder, and if at sea, he would get the help of Poseidon (god of water). You see, all the elements work together to do God's will, for any storm or anything that God wants done. I know that all these angels left heaven on their own, and God does not let them back up to heaven, but as I spoke to all of them, they all still hold reverence to God and know that one day He will destroy all of them, but yet they say, it is His will.

Another thing that I found out that you will not read about in any text is that all twelve gods were present at the birth of Jesus Christ in the manger. They were all present, could not be seen by man, but all were there in attendance. They told me that baby Jesus was glowing when you would look at Him. They say He was a beautiful baby, one without sin. The gods were there with the three wise men and the shepherds to see the baby Jesus.

You see, before Jesus was born, all the gods could appear to man in the flesh. It was since the beginning of time, when the angels decided to come to earth. They came down while Lucifer and God were battling. It was then that they all had relations with the men and women of earth, and they began to have children. These children were half angel and half human. These children would possess angelic powers and be able to control all the elements. So the fallen angels started giving and showing man ancient angelic spells. These spells would later help in the building of the ancient cities and the Great Pyramids. The fallen angels would use spells to move the great rock used to build these wonders of the world. The Stonehenge was another great feat the gods would do and leave for all man to see.

So all through the years before Christ was born, the fallen angels were allowed to appear to man in the flesh. This went on for thousands of years, so they continued to keep having babies through this time. A normal woman would take nine months to give birth, but a goddess would give birth in six months, and they loved to reproduce. So the ancients had many, many children; the angelic bloodline would continue even to this day. These children of this bloodline would still have angelic powers that are in their blood, but it would take them to know who they are and a great deal of meditation to learn and control these powers. Some of the bloodline that is alive would be very powerful, and one that would have two gods as parents would have tremendous powers. It is Lucifer's child through that very same bloodline that the Antichrist will come. It is Lucifer's child that will be very strong. Lucifer will go to the man that is his son and tell him all there is to know. He will not only tell this person that he is indeed Lucifer's child through the angelic bloodline but also help him learn his powers, and Lucifer will coach and add to this person's powers. Lucifer's son will deceive many to believe that he is Jesus Christ by performing all kinds of miracles and showing man his powers and proclaiming that he is the Messiah and is Jesus Christ. This will be the Antichrist.

So once Jesus came into the world, the gods were not allowed to appear before any man. If they would appear before man, they will be destroyed by God. The gods now live on Mt. Ararat near Greece. It is on this mountaintop only where they can appear in the flesh to one another. The Greeks were able to see the gods in the flesh back then. It was a Greek man that took them before council and had them show what all the gods could do. It was the Greeks that believed very strongly in the fallen angels, and it was the Greeks that would give them all their names that we know them by today. They would have sex with all the Greeks, and the Greeks would worship them. Temples that were built to the gods long ago stand today. Many gods have a statue or a temple just to a certain god to worship them. All the gods are very fond of all the Greeks because it was they who had the strongest belief in them.

I know that the fallen are spoken of in the Bible very little, but they have a huge role in the earth's interest. It is God that put them over and in the jobs that each one has. Each job they do is very important and must be carried out, all to the will of God.

The next god, and the last of the gods, that I will speak to is the god of agriculture. She has a very important role. She will look after all our food growth and make sure everyone will eat.

> I am Demeter, the god of agriculture. I chose agriculture to feed everyone and keep them alive, and God must make them eat. I help with the planting of the food, and I make sure that it grows. A war between the gods means famine. I must touch every plant that brings forth food.
>
> A famine is when something's wrong with the plants. Sometimes when the plants are destroyed, it is because of man's greed. That would be planting too soon and trying to grow two crops at once. People eat too much. It was during the fourteenth century that man started becoming obese. People blame society for their bad eating habits.
>
> Chemicals are used to grow things where things should not grow, and even trying to grow things in the cold. People don't know how to grow things. Old people farm still, and the youth wants

a career other than farming. The food inspectors do not do a good job. Too many chemicals in the food, our chicken farms are very unclean.

Peanut butter holds its chemicals, and there are a lot of chemicals in it. Cabbage is a good food. It needs no chemicals and does not hold them. The food and drug inspectors get paid, but not to do their jobs. They don't go to the fields. The government will not allow replacement of irrigation needs, which will and does contaminate our food.

Heaven was a beautiful place. There was lots of singing, and there are places to go [rooms] where you can make the room anything that you want it to be. You can even have any animal you want with you in these rooms. There are no limits. I miss heaven so much. I wish that I never left. I tell you, once you get there, never look back!After speaking with all the gods, all twelve gods, I have a different way of thinking and a more understanding of all the gods. I spoke to each and every one of them as an individual, learning about the earth's past, how the pyramids were built, and all the wonders of the world. Each god offered so much information. It was incredible just to know that each one of them knew God and was in heaven and experienced it, really lived there. It was just that one day, they all decided to come to earth. They all mingled with the people of earth and had children with them. A goddess that would get pregnant would be pregnant for only six months, then give birth, unlike our women taking on a nine-month term. And the healing process for them would only take hours after giving birth to a child. They could literally have the child and the next day be up and around, even having sex again. This is why each god had hundreds of children. They would sometimes find a mate, fall in love, and just keep reproducing again and again, and then mate with other men. There are six male and six female gods. This was decided by God to keep everything equal.

These gods were seen flying through the air back then. They were allowed to appear before man. Aphrodite has a falcon she rides through the air. It will seat three people comfortably. Athena has a winged horse that she rides, Pegasus. She is a warrior, the god of war. Hermes just flies through the air from destination to destination; he is the god of business. Zeus rides the wind. He is the god of all the weather, and he controls it, even the lightning. Poseidon is the god of water and is in control of all water and works with Zeus to make and control all the storms.

As I have spoken to all the gods, it is not uncommon to have these gods as visitors in my house, just a few guests that like to return and talk with us. We know that these gods are the ones who can possess a body because you see they once had a body and crave to feel the flesh even today. The goddesses—Demeter, Hestia, Aphrodite, Athena, Hera—all have come to me in the night. These goddesses are also known as sex demons or the Succubus. It is not like a demon you think. Remember, these goddesses are all fallen angels, and they crave the sex that they once had on earth. It is not uncommon for them to possess your wife, girlfriend, or mistress. They have done so many times over and over again. Sometimes they will even tell you who they are, maybe a drunk girlfriend or wife or one that sleeps. It is at this time when they can possess. They will often reveal themselves, but no one believes them as to who they are. I say believe, because they are very real. I have had sex with them all as they came to me and my girlfriend and possessed her during the night.

Talking with the goddesses is amazing. It is like nothing you can imagine when you know whom you are speaking to. The sex is very wonderful, and the personalities are all different as they are each a different god. It is after the sex that is really interesting, as they will answer questions as I would ask, things that no other man would know. It is all about believing, believing that they truly exist. They are very knowledgeable about heaven, current events, and the history that they know and carry. Just think in bed with you is a goddess that the Greeks worshiped and that was an angel and still is, but fallen. They can offer advice and wisdom they have, if only we ask.

Almost all the goddesses have told me that they have had sex with many stars (actors), and the stars were told as the goddesses revealed themselves to them, but none believed. One star that all the goddesses loved to be with was Johnny Depp. They told me that they would possess his girl, whomever he was with for the night or so, have sex with him, and tell him whom they really were, but he just passed it off. That was just one story they shared with me. Another story is that Hestia and Athena possessed a girl that Brad Pitt was with when he was younger, before he was married, and had sex with him. You see, the goddesses have been doing this for many, many years.

Zeus is the god over all the gods. He is in control. There is but one over him that he answers to; that is Lucifer. Lucifer is over Zeus and all the gods and goddesses. If Zeus can't handle them, then Lucifer is called in to take action, and none of the gods want this to happen. The gods hold council meetings to cover all topics of the world that need addressed. Perhaps God has given some orders for the gods to carry out, maybe to start a war, cause some natural disaster, a massive fire, or flood, or an earthquake. All the gods are kept up to date with their jobs that God has given them. Demeter must touch all growing crops and watch over agriculture.

Lucifer will attend a lot of these meetings as it is his responsibility to watch over them. If a possession that one of the gods is involved in goes bad or they just don't want to leave, Lucifer will go and make sure that they come out of the body. As it is only the twelve that can possess, because they know what it was like to have a body at one time, so it is now that they crave the touch and feel of flesh. When they have these meetings, normally they are all seated and in the flesh at their meeting place on Mt. Ararat. When Lucifer is present, they all must stand or just float because Lucifer is present. Usually Lucifer will just fly and circle them; he never sits.

During the time of a possession, it is not uncommon that the person they wish to possess will climb the walls and ceilings. At this time, claws will come out of their fingers and toes. It is with these claws that they will climb the walls. Their voice will change during the time of possession also. We must keep in mind that all posses-

A GUEST IN MY HOUSE

sions must be cleared or given orders from God. They can't just go possessing bodies and tear them up at will. It is usually only the evil man that will receive such punishment, maybe a killer or one that hurts children. It is then that God gives a green light for the gods to possess to kill. They can have the person that they possess kill and also have them kill themselves. So many possessions are written off as someone that just goes crazy and loses their mind, or maybe that person will have multiple personalities because there is more than one person or spirit inside that body.

If we look back to the Bible, we can remember a possession that Jesus Christ sent the evil spirits out of the body. The person that was possessed was walking through the graveyards and was cutting himself with rocks and stones. It was when Jesus asked the name of the spirit that was in the body that the demon gave the name Legion, "Because we are many." If we remember, Jesus cast the evil spirits from the man's body into a bunch of swine that went into the sea. Well, we now know that the demon Legion was really Lucifer. It was Lucifer that was calling himself Legion, and this is just one of the many other names that Lucifer would use in reference to himself in the Bible.

I had asked Lucifer to come back so I may speak with him again regarding the gods, just to get an overview of how they chose their sex and what they would be god over. It was an interesting conversation with him as always. He revealed so many things about the gods to me, and we also discussed the Illuminati, their origin, and their presence in the world. So you will now read what Lucifer had to say to me about the gods and the Illuminati.

> Because I was of a higher order of angels, I was over the gods before they were gods. [The higher level of angel, it was these angels that got to pick first of what sex and what they wanted to be god over. First was Zeus, Apollo, Athena, Hera, Aphrodite, Hephaestus, Poseidon, Ares, Artemis, Hestia, Demeter, and Hermes. This was the order they took as far as what they wanted to be as in sex and what they were to be god over. Zeus was next in line after Lucifer for power.] There was

no argument amongst the gods, only Zeus and I. I gave them their jobs as I was told from God. Some gods are more free to do their jobs as they want. I have the power to watch over them, to keep them in line, and to make sure that they do their jobs. If a god gets out of line, I will send demons with them, and also they will get extra work from me, and also there would be places that they want to go but are now forbidden.

I am the messenger from God to the gods, and at this point, I would speak to Zeus as he is over the rest of the gods. Zeus would carry out the commands from me.

The gods are at will to whom they want to possess, unless God says otherwise. At this point, God instructs them whom to kill, of evil men, but sometimes they can go off on their own, but they will be punished.

Zeus calls most of the meetings, but any god may call for a meeting if necessary. These meetings are for them to check in and discuss any problems that arise, and also the meetings are for Zeus to give out new projects for the gods. When I call for a meeting, it is usually for a punishment or special message from God. I make my meetings short and sweet, so I have their full attention. For instance, at one of our meetings, Athena was punished. At the meeting, she was to step away from her area and move to the center of the circle. Then I tell her what her punishment is, and then she has the option to answer to her punishment. Then each of the gods has a chance to make a comment, and then she has to accept her punishment, or fight with a response. Once she accepts, it is locked in, and she must agree to do what she said she would do. If she does not, she comes back for a harsher punishment, and then she becomes bound to it, without escape.

Only problems I have are from a few, such as Zeus, really wanting to hear from God, but most hear from me. No problems from Apollo, Demeter, Hermes, Artemis, and Poseidon; the rest are a challenge. Over all, the gods are good and they listen.

The Illuminati is a secret society. This group created the Free Masons. This group was founded in Europe in the middle 1700s. They were a secret society created by the Germans. They were a group of advanced scientist studying mostly chemicals and ways to control people's minds. This would later aid Hitler in his struggle for world power. This started out as a drug that would be shot into people. Some of it has become secret phrases that run through your mind over and over again, or brainwashing (anything that is repeated).

Most power leaders are Illuminati. This is a white supremacy power. The black people of the world (powerful) are trying to mock the power control of the Illuminati. This group started of worshiping God as a Luther religion. They hid behind this religion. The things that they think they can do, like complete mind control, they can't. Hitler is a perfect example of how an Illuminati can control the people of the world. Our US government is Illuminati, with the exception of our current president and John F. Kennedy. All the presidents came from the exact same religion. There are reasons for the two presidents that aren't. The reason is because there needed to be major changes in the world at these times, and someone else had to take the blame or be a distraction. A lot of your history books will say that they are no longer in existence, but they still strive and live.

Ever wonder about a witch? What can they do, what do they do? Are they evil? Is the community of witches very large, and who practices the craft? Or even, who are these witches? Well, you would never guess who practices the craft and who doesn't. This is like a secret society also. Some are born into the craft, meaning the mother was probably a practicing witch, and some just get into it, looking for something or just curious. These women that practice are usually very good with knowing plants and herbs due to the fact that they make potions and need this plant knowledge for this purpose.

So what are their powers? Can they fly? Can they turn people into toads? Can they curse me? Do they talk with the devil? These are all questions I think that many of us think we know, but don't.

A coven. What is a coven? A coven is a group of women that meet secretly, seeking powers from the earth, Mother Nature, and Lucifer. Some of these women help others that seek help for their lives, such as love being number 1, then powers to move things, and learning to do magic. This group of women usually all have a common interest in something, like a better way of life or an easy way out. A lot of the women are looking for a religion that they can believe in, like Wicca, because they are tired of the conventional religions. Another thing is that the group that might be looking to meet Lucifer has a better chance as a group, as if there are eight or more, Lucifer might show up for them, as opposed to just an individual. Many times Lucifer will appear to the girls if he thinks that he can get something from them. Over all, this group is about learning things that no one else believes in, like the supernatural, demons, angels, and Lucifer, but all must have a belief in God.

Now we will read about witches and demons. I have spoke to many witches that have passed on. I have their stories that I think you will find very interesting. They will tell us of their lives both while they were alive and after they have passed on. We will learn what the powers are and the things that they have done. All these stories are true.

I'm Tina. I was thirty years old when I passed. I am a witch. I was not born a witch that I know of, but I met a gal in high school who was a witch. She and I became very good friends. I started spending a lot of time over my friend's house. So my friend would show me how to do things. She was teaching me the craft. My friend was very good at spells that would move things. We would sit and make up our own spells for hours. Once, my friend took me in the summertime to a gathering of witches. I met many witches and got to see many interesting things. Some of the witches did a lot of really dark magic. I didn't like the dark magic that they were doing. There were dog sacrifices [animals], and I got to hear many of their stories about what they had done. I did not believe the stories of how they spoke to Lucifer. I wanted to talk to him on my own, to see if the stories were true. I would sit in my room with my crystal ball for energy, and then I started chanting or singing, asking for Lucifer to come. After I chanted for him a couple of weeks, I got together with my friend, and her and I started chanting together, then he showed up as a man. We spoke to Lucifer. He said that he had been hearing my chant for a very long time, but he didn't show up because I didn't truly believe. He said that the two of us together brought a stronger belief. When he appeared, he gave us additional powers by touching us. He asked us to do a few things for him. He asked us to gather some specific herbs. This was for spells to use on people that he gave. He said that if we do what he asked, he would give us more powers, but he did not. I'd only seen him one more time, and this time he fucked me.

I got really drunk one night. I was throwing up over the toilet. I collapsed over the toilet and hit my head, then never woke up, and I was just engaged too. I saw my light but didn't go into it because I know that I would have gone to hell, so I didn't go.

I was able to actually speak to a coven of three. They were very interesting to speak with, with many stories I know you will enjoy.

I am Jessica. I passed away in 1932. I was born a witch; it was in my blood. I always practiced witchcraft. I didn't go to school. I stayed home and was taught everything. I am from Massachusetts. As a teenager, I was kept at home a lot, to control my magic. We spent a lot of time in the forest in Canada, my mom, my aunt, and myself. We kept a summer home there, so we could go about our way and do as we want. I could turn animals into things. When I was five years old, I turned a mouse into a tea cup and drank tea out of it, but then my mom made me turn it back into a mouse and let it go.

I met Rachel in the woods when I was twelve years old. We sat talking for about an hour or so, and then a small bird landed on Rachel's shoulders. Her mother sent the bird to tell her come home. That is when I realized that Rachel was a witch too. I told Rachel that I was a witch, and so I showed her a trick. I turned the tree upside down. The roots were in the air, and the leaves were on the ground, then I flipped it back to normal. Rachel had to go, so we parted ways, but we agreed to meet back at the same spot every day. We spent the whole summer together. Soon we would spend every summer together until we were eighteen years old.

When we were eighteen, we took a trip to New York. We were meeting with a group of witches to make some friends. We found Cathleen. She seemed to have distanced herself from the group that was there. We invited her to come with us out to dinner. After dinner, we went back to our hotel, and then we asked Cathleen to show us what she could do. At first, she was shy, but we knew that she was stronger. So she started moving things around the room for us. That was good, but we wanted something more powerful. So suddenly Cathleen made a car appear in the room, so then we put the car back on the street.

We flew a lot. Our longest flight was across the ocean. We flew from Massachusetts to Scotland. It took us about nine and a half hours. We flew in for a witches' convention. We stayed for a month, having lots of fun. The men there were very horny. So we were at a pub, and we took two brothers home with us. We kept them for a few nights. We had a lot of fun with them. We showed them witchcraft. We made things move and made things appear. That's how we got our food to the room.

So when we all got back to the States, we lived at Jessica's. We didn't have jobs. Our families took care of us. We were twenty-four years of age at this time. We had a lot of fun in my house. We would make our own spells and potions, and we grew our own weed.

We made a potion we all drank that would kill us. We wanted to make sure that we all stayed together in the afterlife. Rachel was dying, and we tried to save her but couldn't. So we all decided to die with her so we all could stay together. The potion that we made put us to sleep, so there was no pain as we passed on together. We believed that we all would be spirits, so we waited for each other to appear to each other, so we all could see one another. We have had as much fun dead as we had when we were alive.

We went to the witches' convention. There were spirits there watching as we were, and they told us how to get here. There seemed to be a pattern in your energy field, a special energy that we could absorb, so we came to find out what it was. We have been visiting your energy field for about ten years now. We all drank the potion in the winter of 1932 and passed on.

My name is Breanna Stafford, and I am a witch. I died in November of 1938. I was twenty-seven years old. I was born in a very poor little town just outside Oklahoma City. I was born to a young woman that was not married. They kept my birth a secret. They kept me hidden for many years. They didn't want to lose their position on the farm. When I was seven years old, I caught the house on fire. I was very, very angry I was not allowed outside and tired of being kept inside. There was a small candle on the table. I sat for hours, imagining that the flames were shooting to the ceiling. Then the candle fell over, and everything was on fire. I caused the fire and knocked the candle over without moving. I ran from the house, and I ran to the guy closest to the field. I told him that the house was on fire. He asked me who I was, and I told him that it didn't matter. So I ran very far away, and I ended up in a church. I spent the night there. I didn't think that they would ever look for me, but in the early morning, they found me. After that, my mother and grandmother sent me farther away to go live on another farm. They had told me that I was just like my father and that I would never be the same as them.

I did go to live on this farm. They were friends of their family, I think. I anticipated it would be a living hell as before, but it was not. It was wonderful. They had me working in the kitchen with their servant. It was fun. She taught me all kinds of things about cooking, and it turned out that I was very good in the garden. I stayed there, doing anything that I wanted after my work was done. I started talking to the animals and then hearing them talk back. The servant I worked with noticed the things that I could do, and she asked me if I was a witch. I told her that I didn't know what I was, so she took me to a meeting. She told me that she was not a witch but knew of one in the area. She wanted me to meet her and her group of women.

I met them at their meeting and started learning more about witchcraft. The women of that circle taught me everything that I know. I had many natural gifts that I did not know about. They were very impressed with me.

When I was twenty-one years old, I moved out, and I moved to New York. I went there with a guy that was passing through our town. New York was big and exciting. I loved it! I never left New York again. I married this guy, and I met other witches and continued to practice. While I was with the coven, Lucifer appeared to me as in true form and then as a man. He didn't talk much. He asked if we wanted anything special from him.

So after I got married, I lived my normal life and practiced when I could. I had fun in my life. Me and my husband tried to have children, but lost two of them, but I got pregnant a third time and asked for help to carry the baby full term from my coven and Lucifer. The baby came out fine, but I died the next day. Lucifer collected.

When I died, I saw the light. No one was there for me in my light. I had known how to travel already. My coven had talked to spirits, so I knew what to expect upon death, so I knew how to travel.

In my travels, the first place that I went to was India. I wanted to see the great castles and emperors and the beautiful, romantic side of India I read about in books, but it didn't exist. Then I visited the Great Wall of China. I spent a lot of time in the mountains of China with the Buddhist monks. I went to a small island in Indonesia. There was a tribe there that practices a sort of witchcraft. They pray to Lucifer, and he appears. I stayed with them for a while and watched them. They were interesting. Of course,

I would stop in and check on my child once in a while. I visited old witches practicing an old craft. They had different powers that I have never seen. These powers they had, they were calling odd creatures, not knowing that they were demons.

I would like to leave a message for all the living: never make a pact with the devil, unless you have dotted your Is and crossed all your Ts as there is no going back!

I'm Kelly Darsin. I'm a witch, and I died August 15, 1950. I was twenty-one years old. I was born under a full moon, and both of my parents practiced witchcraft. I never had a normal childhood as you might think. My toys were amulets, cauldrons, and wands, amongst other things. I never went to school. My parents homeschooled me. I was taught as a child how to move light. I can shield light also. As a witch, I could do many things. I used to watch the neighbor kids walk down the street. I would cast a spell out to them. They would run into an invisible wall or see a spider or a frog just appear before them. Sometimes I would make their hands and arms move crazy. They would be flapping their arms around and not know why. I also could make potions, but I was not very good at it. My dad would help me try to make potions, but I was no good at it.

As I got older, I was allowed to date boys from church. I had a lot of fun going out with them. I started having sex when I was seventeen years old. The boys thought that I was different looking. I had long straight black hair and very sexy dark eyes. I was five feet seven inches, with small breasts. I met Lucifer once. He came to my house for tea. He appeared as a man, a very handsome man.

I was cursing a boy because he was taking me some place I did not want to go. There were three boys, and they all planned to fuck me. So I went to curse the driver as I was pulled into the backseat, so the spell hit the mirror and came back to me. The curse was to throw the driver from the car, but I got thrown from the car instead and broke my neck and died. At that time, all three boys came and looked at my body. They were all freaking out because they didn't know what just had happened. So when I was standing there, looking at my body, then I knew it was my curse.

My parents knew then I had cursed them and that it came back to me. The curse had left a mark on me that my parents had spotted. My parents were mad that I had done this to myself. They knew that they had taught me better. I stayed and tried to speak to them. I thought that they could hear me. They could not hear me no matter how hard I tried. So after that, I just started wandering around.

I saw the light. My aunt and a few people were in the light for me. I didn't go to the light because I was not sure of where I was going. I did believe in God and Satan, so I did not know where I would end up, so I didn't go. So I traveled to London, England. A friend of our family lives there. He is a witch. I watched him for a while, trying to find someone that could feel and hear me. I checked many places to see witches and covens to talk to me, but no luck.

I have been to your energy field twice. It has been years since I was back. So I heard that you were asking to speak to witches, and they said that you could hear and feel us, so I came into your house. I also know that you can send me to the light. I am tired of this world and wandering around. It is pointless.

If I were to leave a message for all to read, it would be that the world is evil, and watch where you throw your curses.

I'm Cassidy Swiss. I died in 1964, October 2. I was thirty-four years old. I'm from Massachusetts. I was surrounded by witch stories my whole life. About one-half of the people that I lived near knew and believed, and the others did not. I always believed since I was a child. I believed in magic and that witches existed. I would hear rumors and stories about different places. When I was fifteen years old, I went on a summer vacation trip with my best friend and the girl's parents. On the vacation, she revealed to me she was a witch. My friend knew that I was interested and that I had been trying my own spells. She revealed to me some simple spells, telling me that she was a witch. She was making things float around in the room. She would also make the music turn itself on and off. I told her that I was very interested in learning everything. She told me that she would teach me. By the end of our two-week vacation, I had learned to move things slightly. I had also learned to talk to higher powers for help. My friend's parents would pray to Athena and Zeus to ask them for things. My friend helped teach me for many years. I learned everything from my friend, but I was never as good as my friend. Although I practiced witchcraft, I never really mastered anything really strong.

The best part of being a witch was going to coven meetings and watching them do all the cool things that they could do. I loved candles, making them light and putting them out. Lucifer showed up at the coven once. He spoke with everyone at the coven. The first time that I saw him, he told me that the sacrifices would equal the power. At that time, I didn't make any sacrifice, but many years later, I called on him to make that sacrifice. I asked for a shorter life to obtain a certain man. I loved this man. My sacrifice made him ask me to marry him. I was thirty years old. So we married; it was okay at first. He really didn't love me, but we stayed together. It wasn't the happy marriage that I had wanted. Then I had gotten very sick, and Lucifer came to me and told me that it is time.

I was lying in my bed, very sick. It was at this time that Lucifer came to me and told me it was my time. He appeared in spirit at my bedside to take me. I was in pain for about ten minutes, then I died. I saw the light, and nobody was there for me. I sat and cried for a long time and felt very sad. At that time, I had wished that I had not made a pact with Satan. I wished that I had done something different with my life other than trying to be such a witch.

I first traveled to the meeting spots where the coven had met. Then it was there that I met a spirit that taught me how to travel. I didn't know what else to do, so I started to travel. Not many people can hear me. I came across a witch in Ireland that could hear me. I told her about my life a little, and I lied to her a little also. I made myself out to be a better witch than what I was. I stayed and spoke to the lady for quite some time. From there, I traveled to a lot of remote places where nobody was, just to be away. I visited tops of mountains, forests, and deserts.

As I wander the earth still, knowing where I will spend eternity, I wish to leave all the living reading these words a message. It is, I want people to learn about Jesus Christ and believe in Him, and don't believe in Lucifer's promises that he makes!

While speaking with these witches, they all seem to have similar stories: do not trust Lucifer! As I look back at these stories, I see that the witches were not specific in asking Lucifer for what they wanted as the deals were made. Leaving out the details of their deals, such as time frames of when he was to come for them. Still, making deals with the devil is very dangerous. One needs to really know exactly what the consequences will be and then consider them for what they are asking for. I guess we should ask ourselves, are the deep desires we have worth the sacrifice?

Remember that these stories are all true as I spoke to the spirits with my medium Faith. Everything that you read, just imagine being the person that you are reading about and try to put yourself in that situation.

> I died in June of 1970, on the twenty-first. My name is Louise. My father was abusive. He would scream and throw things at us. At first, all this happened, but then it got worse the older that we became. The older we got, the more likely he would abuse us worse. He started with my sister. She was older than me. He was sexually abusing her. This started when she was thirteen years old. I found out that this was happening because we shared a bedroom. I used to lie and pray for him to die. Then when I turned thirteen, he started with me. When I was fifteen years old, I killed my father. He was a drunk. I poisoned him with a potion. I used the plants in our backyard. I put the potion in his drinks. He drank most of the bottle, so then it killed him.
>
> I had done some reading about witchcraft at the library. I took witchcraft into my own hands because God was not answering me. I was very angry with God. My senior year in high school, I met another girl that was a witch, and her and I studied the plants together. Then we started practicing the craft using moon cycles, candles, fire, music, dance, and amulets. Our outfits were

worn for different seasons. I started throwing parties at my own place. Sometimes they were teaching parties, worshiping parties, or sex parties.

I never officially joined a coven because I did not want to drink blood, and I didn't want to listen to anyone else's rules either. I was thirty years old when I passed. I had breast cancer. I was diagnosed when I was twenty-eight years old, and then I died two years later. They wanted to take my breast, but I said no. I tried to cure myself with many potions, but none worked.

When I died, I came out of my body, and I was scared. I saw my body lying still there. Then I saw the light, and my sister was in it and she was reaching out to me. I didn't go into the light because I was scared. I thought my sister was in hell. I sat inside of a church for a very long time, thinking about what I am to do and why I am here. I sat there, until one day, an old lady came up to me and started talking. This old lady told me that she had been watching me for months from the back of the church. She told me that I didn't have to stay here, but that I could travel.

The first place that I went to was Paris, France. I stayed there for a very long time. When I left there, I went to Moscow, and then I came back home. I started watching people that I know. I would go and stare at their graves for months. I was wishing that I could have saved her. I was thinking of how to get to my sister and save her. I felt very sad.

Then every now and then, I would travel just to get away—an ocean, mountain, field, on top of a pyramid. I was in fear of the light, thinking the whole time that I was going to hell. Until I met you and Faith, who told me about the light and what was proper. Now I feel like I need to go to my sister so we can be together again.

If I could leave a message for all those living, it would be, people should not ignore child abuse!

I'm from Colorado. My name is Annette Ruffete. I was thirty-one years old when I passed. I was born a witch, and I was ten years old when I realized that I had powers. I used to watch my mom move things but was uncertain of how she was doing it. So my mom sat me down one day and explained everything to me. My mom told me that we are witches and that our family goes back centuries. My blood carries special powers. If I choose to use the powers, she will show me how. I told her that I wanted to use the powers that I had, so she agreed to teach me, but I had to understand that we only use our powers for good. We do not hurt people. I told her that I understand and I would not hurt anyone.

My mom started teaching me everything that she knew. First, she taught me small things, things that can be easily controlled in the house. Like how to move something small and like how to turn lights on and off. She then gave me many books and manuscripts to read. What she gave me was our family history. So I read everything. Some of the things that I read were very interesting and unbelievable. After I read the books, my mom made me promise to keep their secret from everybody that I knew.

I joined a coven when I was like sixteen years old. I wanted to learn more, I knew that there had to be more. Some of the people in the coven were fake. They wanted to do magic tricks, not magic. It was hard to find three other witches that were true. I did find three girls, and we started teaching each other all the different things that we knew. Very soon, we were brewing very erotic potions and levitating. It was a lot of fun! I would be able to fly one mile through the woods where no one could see me. I stayed with the coven the rest of my time. I had made a promise that I couldn't break to my mother. I had promised that I would never hurt anybody with magic, but I did. This was a blood promise. So the power of the magic came back to me because of what I did. I killed someone. I made them have a car accident. I knew them. It was a guy that hurt me, so I killed him. I lifted his car over a cliff. Three days later, I was dead. I sat up in my bed. I was trying to breathe, and I saw the swirls around my head. My mom sent her voice and told me, "Why did you do this? You now know what is coming! You were warned. You knew the consequences. Good-bye, my daughter." So she left me, and I fell dead on my bed. I saw the light but knew not to go because I would go to hell. I died in 1982 of February. It was very cold.

It is very boring and lonely. No one talks to us. It is sad knowing you will be in hell.

I would like to give all the living a message: Don't make promises that you can't keep, but keep all the promises that you make. Do not break them! While talking to these witches, we were also allowed to speak with some of the five hundred angles that left heaven also (the five hundred fallen). These were the angels that took Lucifer's side when God and Lucifer were fighting. I thought it would be very interesting to speak with these angels, just to get their thoughts on everything, like why they left heaven, their jobs on earth, and whom they like to torment. We will find out what the world was like and how they control things now on earth. We will be talking to more witches as we move forward also.

I am one of the five hundred angels that followed Lucifer out of heaven. My name is Zoni. Everything was good in heaven. Lucifer thought he was as equal as God; that is why God cast him out. We came down after their battle in heaven. God told us that we all had to choose what side we were to be on from now until the end. Lucifer wanted one thousand angels, but God said no… only five hundred. God named me Zoni.

I do whatever Lucifer tells me to do. My free will means I can go wherever I want on earth. One demon every week is assigned to take reports from watchers, which are other demons that are sent to get Lucifer. Lucifer needs me to help drag souls to hell. It must be one of the five hundred to drag a soul to hell. The light is the dividing factor between heaven and hell. Most get a chance to wait for judgment or go through the light now. So when the person dies, that has been really bad, they do not get a chance to go to the light or not, but they are dragged straight through the light, straight to hell. When they come through the light on their way to hell, four demons are there to take them to hell. For those who disobey the rules of after-death, they will have two options. One is to go to the light, and the other is to continue breaking the rules and become an evil spirit.

I am about four feet tall. I have a set of regular angel wings, no hair on head. I am in a man's image with wings. Angels have no sex, male or female. I can move anything that I want. The biggest thing that I moved was the London Bridge. I moved the bridge just enough to be offline with the road in (1982). I had to move it back within a couple of days because I got in trouble with Lucifer. It was fun to mess with the English people. They are confused easily.

I want to tell all the humans, if they would believe more in God and His Son more, they would not have to complain about the evil as much.

I followed my friends from heaven—my name is Amacki—when they all came down. When we all got to earth, we just followed Lucifer's instruction. I would get to torment the humans that I was jealous of. I got freedoms here that I did not have in heaven. I like to get kids in trouble. It's very easy to do, between ages of three to ten years old. I mess up their rooms after they clean them, and then their parents make them clean their rooms again. Lucifer yells at me a lot, because he says I don't listen.

I usually don't kill. I will mess up their speech and get in their minds and make them forget what they were doing or saying. I like to work with other of the fallen angels. I do not regret leaving heaven. Work in heaven would be cleaning up after the dead humans that are having fun. God wants everything to be neat and tidy, so we clean up after the humans.

The biggest things that I have moved were some trees to place into people's way, but I have moved many things inside of people's homes.

We are now preparing for Armageddon. We have to learn our spells and practice listening to Lucifer from far away. Our throwing spells, that is one of our main offenses. We are being taught to listen to the sounds that will call us to be ready for battle.

My name is Tyco. I left heaven because it sounded like fun, something different. I was in heaven for like three thousand years before I decided to leave. I get to kill, but only when Lucifer tells me to do so. I killed yesterday, a crazy old man in Florida. I made him crash his car into the river. I have killed presidents in other countries, and I have killed a woman in a dark house. She suffocated.

I still have my wings, and I still fly solo when I can. It took me one hour to get from Sicily to Seville, Ohio. I do regret leaving heaven, but I did what I did. I wait to get my orders from Lucifer. They come at random. I am mostly in Europe more than anywhere else.

I'm four feet four inches tall, very short hair. I am white. I play the harp and the flute.

When I saw Christ at the manger when he was born, I knew it was time for a big change. Christ's birth meant humans had to believe to go to heaven. I think that humans that don't believe are very foolish.

I do have power over evil spirits. I can tell them what to do and when. I can use them to kill and do as I will.

I want to tell all those who read this that the Bible is True!

I am Klev, one of the five hundred angels that left heaven with Lucifer. I had a chance to leave heaven, so I did, to do something different. I never had a chance before. I always had to do as God said. I thought this would be something of an adventure, and it is definitely an adventure. Before I left heaven, God told me that I was not allowed back. I serve Lucifer in hell [lake of fire]. In hell, I manage a group of peopleI manage a group in hell of people that have been murdered, that were bound for hell, just that their time came up quickly.

For now, people are sent to the lake of fire, in the center of the earth. The souls are in a very hot place. The area that I occupy is very unstable. The ground shakes very often. The people in this lake of fire are held to a spot where they stand and can't move. No walking around at all. Very few scream, and they can only move their heads to look around. When they look around, they see pointy rocks facing up [stalagmites] only when a flash of fire burst or when a new person is brought in. Other than that, they only see utter darkness. All those in hell can see all those standing next to them. All are very close together without touching each other.

The people in hell [lake of fire] are tortured with the thoughts of what they could have had if they only believed in Jesus Christ. They are also being reminded of the horrible things that they did to other people on earth. No one knows anybody in hell, no friends. Your mom could be standing right next to you, and you wouldn't even know it. Sometimes these people fall down, and I have to pick them up. A lesser sin could mean less heat and less flames, or a smaller sin could mean no heat and no flames. People with no sins of a serious nature would feel no heat. People do slide right into the lake of fire [feet first]. It is like a sliding board, where the people land feet first, very hard. I myself sometimes will appear to those dying and take them to hell. I will tell them, "You are going to hell. It is my job, and I will take you there." I would tell you, "I do not want to drag you to hell, so believe!"

I am one of the five hundred angels that left heaven. My name is Forcus, and I left heaven because I was bored. I don't like rules. When I went to work for Lucifer, I asked him what he needed help with, and Lucifer told me that he wanted my help deceiving people and bringing them to him. Over the course of the years, it has been the Catholic Church that has been deceived the most, because they have been around the longest. The biggest deceiver is to bring in false idols. You can then deceive in masses. I'm responsible for bringing in the statues of the saints and using them to deceive people. I am also bringing in false prophets to deceive. Like preachers that say they can heal, this takes the focus off of God and Christ, and people that say they see Mary, making them worship Mary instead of Christ. I make them see Mary, and it is a deceit. It is great to bring deceit to people that have never known about God, for when they learn about Him, the deceit is already planted. Remember, when you are deceived, there is a reason behind it.

Tradition is another huge deceit, such as going to church and saying prayers repetitive, saying the words without realizing their meanings, being forced to do something, like parents making their kids read the Bible and go to Sunday school. Also the people that scare other people using their Bible. Propaganda, which is very big in the field of politics, like phrases and words that most people are unfamiliar with. Our government, which says, "We will do this now," when in actuality it takes several years for them to do. When a law is written, it may be for one thing, but it contains many others, contains many other laws that are hidden within this one law.

I was the one that deceived you when you were speaking to the angels from heaven. You were to talk with two angels, when you only spoke with one. I was acting as the second angel and deceived you, only to have you believing me after a few minutes before you realized the deceit.

After talking to a couple of the five hundred fallen angels that left heaven, I was very interested in speaking to more of them. It seems that they all have jobs for Lucifer as he appoints them to them from the fall. Some have jobs in hell (lake of fire), and some on earth to do as he wants. As I spoke to Klev about the lake of fire, he was giving me a full picture of the way part of things look. It was also chilling to know that the people were standing all the time, not able to move, but I did ask him a question. I asked if he missed heaven, and he responded, "Yes, and I wish I never left."

So many people do not believe in Jesus and maybe think life after death is crazy. All we simply need to do is have a belief in Jesus. Time and time again, the spirits that have passed on and the angels tell us to just believe. It was true that I was deceived on the talk with Forcus, the deceiver. That night, I was to speak with two angels, when I only spoke to one. He slipped in to deceive me. It was only after I started to speak to him that things didn't add up. It was then that he revealed himself to me. This was a test to me, to try the spirits and be sure of whom I am speaking with. Such as I was tested, so are many others and just don't know it but go on being deceived.

> I was twelve years old when I started reading the stories of the Salem witches. I asked my mom if I could be a witch for Halloween that year, because I had to write a paper about what I wanted to be for Halloween [the character]. Because I was so interested in the witches, I did research that I didn't have to do. I wanted to speak with a real witch, so I ran an ad in the local newspaper: "Looking for a local witch to talk to for my school paper." One week after it was in the paper, I received a phone call. The lady told me that she would meet with me at the local library, so I met her there. We had a very long conversation. She told me of her life as a witch and told me her name was Hilda, and I told her mine was Beth. She wore a skull necklace, and I told her that I too wanted to be a witch. She said true witches are born, but I could still practice. After that, all I wanted to do was to be a witch. Hilda gave me her number and told me, when I came of age,

that she would help me if I still wanted to be a witch.

I became obsessed with witchcraft. If I wasn't at school or doing something for Mom or Dad, I was studying witchcraft. By the time that I was eighteen years old, I had memorized everything that involved witchcraft that I could find. I took a trip into Salem when I graduated. I then spent one month there, talking to witches. I think a lot of the things that I was told there weren't true. So I called my friend that I met a long time ago [Hilda]. I met up with here, then she started to teach me to do things instead of memorizing words. I was not very good at first. Hilda then introduced me to another girl, and there was an opening in her coven, so I joined the coven. My friend called upon Lucifer in the coven. We called once, and he appeared. They told him that I was the new girl and that I needed to be initiated. He put his hand on me, and it burned. He told me he could give me anything that I wanted, for a price. I asked him what kind of things that I could give him. He told me that there were many things I could give him, but he told me he really just wanted my soul. I told him that I had to think about it. "But show me what you can give me, like a trial run." He told me to hold out my hands and ask for something. So I held out my hands, and I asked for a pizza. So okay, then I was holding a pizza from a local pizza shop. "That was good," I told him. "Now let's try for me to move a tree." I knew the spell in my head, so he told me, "Go ahead and try." I did, and the tree moved, I knocked it over. I told him I would think about it. I asked if he could come back. He replied, "No!" He said, "Decide now." I told him that I would not give him my soul, so he took years off my life, too many. I died when I was thirty-seven years old. I had asked him to give me the power to use all the spells that I knew, so some of the spells worked, and most didn't. The girls told me that I did not believe enough in Lucifer for my spells to work. As much as I tried, they never really worked. I continued to practice and stayed in the coven for a while.

I met a guy. He took me away for a while. We got married. It lasted four years, and then we divorced. I then moved back near my parents' house, I worked and got involved with some of the girls from the old coven, but not too deep. I came home one night after work, and the lights didn't work in the house. Nothing would come on. I found my way to a flashlight and some candles, so I went down to the basement to turn on some of the breakers. When I went down the steps, I tripped and fell, and the next thing I knew, I was dead. A demon came to me after I had passed and told me it was my time to die. I died on March 3, 1957. It was very cold outside.

When I traveled, the first place I went to was London, England. I stayed a few weeks. I had already known how to travel. I learned it from the coven. I traveled all over Europe. I didn't want to go through the light because I was scared, but I did see my great-aunt in the light.

I have been coming to your energy field for about ten years. So finally I was invited in as a guest in your house to give you my story, and now I wish to go to the light and end my travels.

So my medium Faith created the light that Beth had avoided many years ago, but now having the assurance she would go to heaven, she went into the light and met up with her great-aunt.

I was twenty-three years old when I died. I'm Marie. I passed away on July 7, 1957. I was raised by my grandmother, who was a practicing witch. My grandmother taught me how to heal and how to curse things. She also taught me how to fly and how to respect the craft. My grandma believed in keeping our craft a secret. She made me promise not to tell anyone. I never told anyone until after I died. I was in a coven. It was made up of all family. I never married, but I had a boyfriend, and he wanted me to move away from my family. I told him no, so he got angry and killed me. We were arguing outside the building where he worked at. He was almost twenty-five years old. He slammed my head against the brick building. He thought he had just knocked me out, but I was dead.

When I died, I saw my body lying there, then realizing that I was dead, then my thoughts were, "You are going to pay for this!" So I went to see my grandma, and she grabbed her wand and killed him that night. She used a spell. We went to his house. When my grandma killed him, I was standing there with her. The boyfriend says, "What are you doing here?"

Grandma said, "I am here to take you!"

He said, "Take me where? I'm not going anywhere with you, bitch!"

So then my grandma says a spell, then he dropped dead. When he died, I saw his spirit, and I told him, "She was going to take you!"

Then he told me, "How is this possible?"

Then we told him that we were witches. My grandma told me, "Do what you like, but don't go through the light if you think you will go to hell."

So I began to travel. I went to Egypt, where I went into the pyramids. I saw drawings on the walls, some statue, and some coffins also. I also visited China and visited all over. I wanted to see the culture. I went up high into the mountains. The people that live there are very simple. So I went back and talked with my grandma and told her of my travels.

I would like to leave a message to all those reading this: Avoid men; they bring trouble. And listen to your friends, because they speak the truth.So after all, Marie was able to go to the light; my medium Faith created it for her. It was in the light that she saw all her loved ones and was on her way to join them in heaven.

I am the fallen angel Xaphan. When I first came from heaven with Lucifer, I had no job. Every time Lucifer came to get me, I would be hanging around anywhere there was fire. I loved it and always liked it hot. Lucifer came to me one day and asked me if I would help out with some fire problems, because the fire in the lake of fire kept going out. I told him that I would help him. I went with him to the lake, and I spent some time with him, trying to figure out the problems. We had to work against God. Actually, I figured it out, so the problem was that we had to continually open up new holes in the lake, because the old holes would fill up, so the fire could not breathe. So it has become my job to keep the fires burning forever. I am over all of hell to keep the fires burning. I do have some demons to help suck out the holes that fill up with molten lava. Sometimes they are filled with big rocks, and sometimes they must blow off the ground to find the holes so that the fire keeps burning.

The size of hell is very deep and very large. Some areas require more fire than others. So if Lucifer needs me, he calls on me for a particular job to start a fire. So for instance, a forest fire, and usually the fire is used to destroy and hide something. My last fire was in Central America. This took place at the end of Mexico in the year AD 900.

If I think about it, I do miss heaven at times very much. My job in heaven was being a door opener, which meant that I would open doors for you. I would open three or four doors at a time. My job had been to open doors, so when God made the offer and opened the door to earth, I decided this was my time to go through the door.

I never knew that there was a president of hell. This next fallen angel has an important job—she is the president of hell. A very interesting story she has.

I left heaven because too many of my friends had left, and I was hoping that here on earth that I could be in charge of something. I knew Lucifer from heaven, and I knew that he would give me a job that I could be in charge of. In heaven, although not a God-given job, I always kept my group of angels in order. So when I asked Lucifer for a job, I told him that I wanted to be in charge of something. At first he kind of pushed me away and told me that he would look for something for me.

One day he came back to me with a job offer. He asked me if I would like to be the president of hell. I would get to keep track of where everybody is at. They report to me weekly with reports, and I get to tell them what to do if they are not doing it right. When something goes wrong, I have to find somebody to fix it. I get the only spot in hell that has no heat. I really like my job a lot. I only must listen to Lucifer. I do get to come to earth every now and then. I possess a person's body when I come out of hell. I love to eat. It is the only reason that I leave hell. I love to eat cakes and pies of all kinds. I also like cheese-burgers, cheesecake, and I enjoy the atmosphere.

I chose to be female when I first came to earth, because they were much better looking. I was in heaven around six thousand years before I decided to leave.

I would tell all that read this book, it's very hot down here. Join me!

This next witch is of something a little different. Usually, all the spirits would come to me and tell me their stories. This is a very popular witch of a sort, a local witch. Some know of her grave more than her. The Witches' Ball—this is a local witch from Brunswick, Ohio. You can google "The Witches' Ball" and see all the information the search engine will give. I had known of this grave for a while, so I thought I should go and see if she was around her grave still, or just try to contact her. This is very popular with the young people just dabbling in witchcraft. So I did make a visit to her grave, and it was very powerful to see that upon her grave was a huge granite ball. It was this that gave the grave the name and all its recognition. When I arrived to the grave, I saw all the leftover candles and trinkets of all sorts from a leftover séance. Maybe they were trying to reach her. I placed my hands upon the ball. My medium Faith was with me, so we asked to speak to her if she would come through. She began to speak to my medium, and this is her story—a very interesting one it is.

My name is Hilda. I am stuck under this gran-ite ball. I grew up in Brunswick, but I was born in Pennsylvania. My family moved here when I was less than one year old. It was the year 1918 when I was growing up here. My mother and I were born witches, and my brother also, but he never practiced any magic. My father died when I was just eight years old, and my mother made her living by practicing her witchcraft and letting it be known. People would come from all around to get help from her. When she died, I followed in her footsteps. I was fifteen years old when she died. I was a witch that helped people.

It was 1942 when I was placed under this ball of a grave. I was placed her by one of the girls from my coven. She had gotten angry with me and the rest of the coven because one night we had a meeting without her. She had been practicing some bad things on her own, then we found out. It was then that we decided to get rid of her. She had become very dark in her practice, so we told her that we were going to let her go from the coven. She had become very angry. She told us that she could do great things for us. We told her sorry, but we weren't looking to do dark magic, so she killed us. She killed us with a spell and bound us where we lay. Once she killed us, she then moved us where we are and lie now, under this ball. [Her name was Mary Trighter.] I was twenty-eight years old when I was imprisoned under this ball. I am here with my coven [Sarah and Mary Winde]. We all did see people in our light when we passed. It was that we were unsure of the light and thought we were stuck here under this ball in our graves, thinking that we could never be set free. Until I met you and Faith, I never thought we could leave here, but now I understand we may leave this great prison of the grave.

I have a message that I would like to give to all the living: séances don't work to dead people in graveyards, and if you are going to practice magic, don't practice dark magic.It was at this time that I shared the good news to Hilda and her coven. I had told them that for some reason, I was compelled to visit this grave. I did explain that I was writing a book and told them what it was all about. I believe I was sent here for more than a story. I believe God had a purpose for me that day. It was to set these prisoners free. When I told them today is the day they go to heaven, I felt their energy rise and their presence very known. So one by one, Faith created the light where each one was reunited with their families after being captives for so very long.

I left heaven because the group of angels I was hanging out with all left heaven. My job on earth is to clean up the crap, like creepy people, whores on the street, drug addicts, and alcoholics. When it is time for them to die, I take them if they are going to hell. I take them and drop them into a certain part of hell. I like to visit this part of hell. I think it is funny, because I finally get to get these people off the street and put them into where the most fire is in hell. I am Kee, one of the fallen five hundred angels that left heaven to join Lucifer on earth.

When I see the people that are going to hell, I tell them that they should have listened to whoever was trying to help them. I also tell them that Jesus is real, but they don't get to see Him. Lucifer tells me and sends me to those whom I am to take.

My name is Maurice. I was born a witch. My mother and grandma were witches. The witches go as far back as I can remember. We came over here from Ireland in 1830. My father was not a witch, but he allowed the practice. We are often something like the storybook witches. We practiced dark magic, no covens. We kept it in our family. I grew up in a small house in Pennsylvania. We grew all our own food. We never left the land, although my father did. He would go to work. I had one brother, who showed no signs of magic, which disappointed my mother, until he brought the neighbor's house down. He was very mad at the neighbors and thought about setting it on fire, then it happened.

My father would bring home a cat once a week. We would place a spell on the cat, then we would send the cat to a certain person or place, and then the cat would release the spells. We sent the cat with a hush [quiet] spell to the local lady that owned the grocery store. When she touched the cat, it attached the spell, then the lady couldn't talk anymore. When we would send a spell very far away, we used an owl to deliver it.

We used to lure small children to our house (under five years old). We would use them for spells, the innocence of their eyes, the blood, and use the bones to get their youth. We made medicine with them also.

I died because I became old. No one left to take care of me. I was eighty-two years old when I died. I saw the light—it was a blinding light. An angel came to me at that time. He told me I can go through the light or stay as a spirit on earth. After that, I traveled everywhere. Traveling is nice because I don't have to stay in one place too long. I have been coming to your energy field for about ten years, but this was the first time that I was asked to come inside the house. I usually travel alone. I died in 1925.

My name is Heather, and I hated my childhood because of too many rules. I grew up in Georgia. When I was eighteen, I moved out to California. The first place that I looked to stay, I found a roommate to stay with, and she was a witch. The place smelled so good I couldn't wait to move in. There were plants and butterflies everywhere, big statues with crystals, all different colors. I moved in and let her teach me. Her name was Kelly. I still see Kelly sometimes. She was a very funny witch. We smoked a lot of pot. We spent a lot of time being mischievous. She taught me how to move things. She showed me how to change my appearance and, of course, how to fly. We contacted Lucifer for help to learn to fly.

We would go to a club, pick up a guy and speak with him, say a little spell, and look deep into his eyes. Then we would tell him what we wanted him to do, then suddenly he was asking us to dinner and "Here is my number." I might tell him a sad story, of how I needed money for something. He would give us the money, and then we would go about our way. It was like that a lot.

We went to coven meetings. No dark magic, mostly fun. We would dance naked a lot under the moon. We drank each other's blood and sang a lot of songs and played with the wind.

I died in a car accident. I was driving but a little too high on pot. I drove off a cliff, into the woods. When I saw my light, there was no one there for me. The angel explained the light to me, then I decided to be an earthbound spirit. I died in 1973.

Lucifer has many angels from heaven that followed him to earth from heaven. These angels total five hundred. They are known as the fallen five hundred angels. Lucifer has given each and every one of them a job to do on earth, and he rules over them. I was able to speak with a few of them as Lucifer brought them to me. I have spoken to a few earlier in this book, but now I will speak to several, just to give you an idea of the kind of jobs they do and why they left heaven to come to earth.

I am Cresil. I can make people be lazy in a very bad, constant way. When I'm sent by Lucifer or called on by a few, I can make you be a sinner by doing nothing. I love TV addicts, couch potatoes, filthy do-nothings, and drunks who don't function. I prey on a lot of lazy older men and sloppy people. I help get souls to hell by keeping one's laziness as a mind game to make them not leave the house or not to go to church or visit with too many other people. I can give you a feeling of worthlessness to make sure you don't want to participate in activities or socialize with other people. I also like fat people, and I try to temp people to be fat and gluttons to keep them lazy. These people are easy to get.

I go back and forth to hell and earth a little bit, but mostly on earth. I have a helper demon created by Lucifer to help me, and he can create a smaller demon to keep in someone's house to keep with his tasks. I am an angel, one of the five hundred who left heaven with the rest. I wish to go back to heaven, but I know that there is no hope for that, and besides, I have been very bad here too. I still speak to God, but I never hear back. I did like heaven but left. It was an option I never had before, and I'd seen so many others going. I do miss the comfort and singing. It's hard to find good singers down here compared to the angels up there.

I can possess but usually chooses not to. I think it's odd, and I don't want to hurt people, but only mess with their minds when they are already in a state of laziness and stupid, too.

When I go to hell, I go to a small hole, and it's kind of my home. I don't take people to hell or anything like that. I like Americans. They are the laziest people, then the rich Europeans come next. There are not too many lazy people in the rest of the world, just one here or there, mostly older rich people in other countries. Example, one lazy guy in Florida, he keeps a demon with him, and he is about fifty-two years old, and he lies in bed, watches TV, and has the next-door kid clean once in a while. He orders in all his food and goes nowhere except to the doctors' about once a month. He is going to hell. His name is Samuel Trips. On a lighter note, I have never visited you.

My name is Oriaxes. I will command fights and troops during the battle with Lucifer at the end of time. For now, I teach astrology to other angels, demons, and watchers for all the changes happening around the sky with planets, stars, and meteors, etc.—I watch them all, and I keep Lucifer informed of any changes. I saw a change last night. One of the stars moved farther north [December 21, 2012]. One of the stars disappeared. It is gone and won't come back. Eventually, this will keep happening. Your scientists will not tell the people of these changes. One day, your star will go too (the Sun). This will not be for a while. When it is time, I will get to tell the troops where to position [like the stars]. This will be for the battle of Armageddon. I keep Lucifer informed of different places that come up in the universe, especially the moving clouds in space.

I left heaven because my friend Aphrodite left. My name is Tolian. Aphrodite kept me near and let me help her and told me stories. When Aphrodite came down from heaven first, she would come back to heaven and tell me her stories. When we had the option to come to earth from heaven, I didn't hesitate. I wanted to be with my Aphrodite.

After Christ was born, I had to go my own way. Lucifer assigned me to animals. I work with animals in the Middle East and Europe. I work with sheep and goats. I keep them populated. I still do secret things with Aphrodite. When Aphrodite can't interfere with a love, I can. I may test the love or cause problems for the couple, or bring them closer together.

I'm Cefel, also one of the five hundred that left heaven. I left heaven because lots were leaving, and God was angry. Heaven was scary while God was angry, so I came to earth. When I got to earth, first thing that I did was some exploring. I know where everything is on earth—mountains, rivers, landmarks, cultures and people, and tall trees.

I was in Paris this morning. It is there that I look to kill one person a day. I create accidents where people will die. I hate the French because they killed my girlfriend many years ago [Analee]. She had stolen something from her job. She was a maid, so the government at that time…put her to trial, then killed her. She died stealing food.

I do what is asked of me by Lucifer, mostly fun things, like going to parties, getting people drunk, and encouraging sex and drugs for fun.

My name is Euwu. I left heaven because one of my friends left heaven. I like to knock things over, like buildings and trees. When God or Lucifer need a building knocked over, they call on me. This is what I do for fun. My actual job is to watch ancient tribes. I have been watching these tribes since they formed. Most of them are tribes of protectors. Most of the tribes are protecting a passageway or some form of highly held tribal relics. An example would be the Montinii tribe. They no longer exist in your records. They have been marked as extinct. For example of something that God might have me do, I knocked over a tower in West Africa. It wasn't finished being built, and God wanted it knocked over. I had to do this twice, because they did not listen. A lot of the tribes that I work with are secret. They protect their tribe's secrets, so if some of the secrets were to leak out, it could change the beliefs of history. I also protect the powerful or rare items they do not want found. For the tribes, they hold valuable powers. All of these are just money to regular people.

I helped knock down the Tower of Babel and some of the Egyptian homes, the Egyptian management that were not functioning properly.

I also am one of the five hundred that left heaven. I'm Soot. I left heaven because I wanted to explore earth. I have been exploring earth for over fifteen thousand years. I know it very well. I know all the sand and rock of the earth. I know where everything is at. It is my job for Lucifer. I work a lot with the ocean. So after a hurricane, if any houses, ships, or anything that should not be in the ocean, I cover it up and bury it with sand. I buried Atlantis thousands of years ago. I also have buried many bridges that men have tried to build, especially in the Northwest Passage to dry land. I have helped archeologist to locate and prevent, if needed, certain items of interest. I helped open and close some of the passageways in the pyramids.

Some of the larger things that I have buried were islands that never made your maps and large ships, anything that has fallen into your sea.

I too am one of the five hundred angels that left heaven. I am GyLou. I left heaven because sometimes it was too noisy. I like silence. That is the only reason that I have for leaving. I would go back if I could.

Here I often sit in solitude on top of mountains. I was given a job by Lucifer that I enjoy.

My job is to stop reproduction, to cause women not to be able to have children. I will give them miscarriages, stillborn death, and crib death, all after birth within the first year. I like to kill children that could possibly change the world. Sometimes I kill the baby before it's born to save the mother, because the mother might die during the birth. These are the women that should not have children. After the baby is born, it is hard to kill it. If I kill the child, I take it to hell, then it is taken from hell by an angel to heaven.

I dislike all the singing by the angels in heaven. Angels have a choice to obey or disobey God, but have no soul. So when disobedient, God punishes.

I love silence. I go to the mountains and deserts to be alone. I only leave when Lucifer calls me away.

I left heaven because I liked Lucifer, and I wanted to be with him. I'm Valac. I work with magic and used to work with dragons. I had a chance to work with Lucifer, so I left heaven, and he gave me a job. Lucifer assigned me to help those magic people. I bring them things from the earth that they might need, like birds, cats, snakes—anything they might need. I help those that do magic and especially those who perform in front of others. It was much more popular years ago, so sorcerers were kept by the kings to aid in life and battle.

I would bring things to the witches that could hear me and aid in their magic, for all those born with natural powers [magic]. I'm working on bringing all the animals and magical people together at the final battle.

I can possess magical people to help them in their magic by knowing what they need to further their powers. I can help them in ways they don't know they need help in.

I'm Lilly. I left heaven in hopes of helping earth. I am also one of the five hundred. I wanted to make earth more peaceful by bringing more songs and more flowers. Lucifer lets me help people make beautiful music. I help churches with writing their music and lyrics. So when people need help in music, I help them with solos, groups and choir, and their music director.

I also help with floral arrangements in hospitals, homes, funerals, and churches. I help with the gods. I get them music and help decorate. I work with Aphrodite on some things. I help her pick the best flowers or find music, if they need music or for a wedding that Aphrodite might be helping out on. I worked with all the gods since the beginning.

I have helped many groups in the music industry, like the Oak Ridge Boys, Amy Grant, Vince Gill, the Statler Brothers. I helped them by bringing inspiration to the artist.

I am Makel, one of the fallen five hundred. I left heaven because I liked Lucifer and some of my friends left also.

I love to swim in the ocean. I like sharks, and I can speak to them. I like octopus also, the ones that tell ancient stories. They all tell me what is happening in the sea and of all the changes. The largest octopus I have seen is twelve feet in diameter [its head] and has forty feet tentacles. This creature would take out any big ship passing its way. The one I speak of is in the Pacific north waters. There are maybe seven that big in the world. I monitor changes in the waters from the two animal stories.

I also find unique creatures on earth to tell me stories as well. An example would be palaeeudyptes, dragons, turtles, and tortoise— these creatures live very long. My job is to gather stories of all the animals and report to Lucifer. I spoke with some crocodiles yesterday. They are tired of disappearing, man taking them. Their bones are used for dark magic, and their skins are very valuable. They worry that they will no longer be around. They are located in Africa. The land has disappeared also for them to live on. The less land, then the crocodiles will pick up a disease, because too many of them living in a small area. The land is changing also, no more water or trees.

This next fallen angel you will read about wants to go back to heaven very badly. I have spoken to a lot of these fallen angels, those of the five hundred. It is this angel that gets my attention the most. I just can't imagine living in heaven and then getting tired of it so much that I want to leave. You see in the stories you have read that all had similar reasons for leaving heaven. They all had friends that left, or they just wanted to be with Lucifer. It seems, after so many years that have passed, that a majority wish they could reclaim God's grace and return to heaven, but none that I spoke to have pleaded more than the angel you are about to read about. His name is Leapie. He is one of the fallen also but wishes he never left.

I'm Leapie, one of the five hundred that left heaven. I left heaven because my female companion left heaven. I really was unsure of leaving heaven. I do wish from time to time that I never left heaven. I believe heaven was better. I try to get as close as I can to heaven to see, but I never can see. I try to communicate to angels and God. I have spoken to the archangel Gabriel at times. I try to tell her to tell God just how sorry that I am. She always listens to me but never tells me anything good. I will keep trying.

My job for Lucifer is...I watch babies in hospitals and where they are born. I'm protecting them from people that might hurt them by mistake [parents and caregivers].

The fallen angels, or the five hundred that left heaven, we know that they all have jobs for Lucifer to do here on earth. Every one of them has a different job to do. Some are in hell, taking care of things, and some are here on earth. All these angels made a choice some fifteen thousand years ago, and now they live with that choice. You see that angels do have a choice to make, and if they disobey God, then they are punished.

The first of the angels that left heaven were only twelve, and these twelve would be able to go back and forth from heaven to earth as they pleased. These angels would be better known as the gods (Greek gods). It was because of this that God was getting fed up with everything. So while the twelve were traveling back and forth and then staying at times on earth, Lucifer and God were fighting, fighting so badly that angels were getting away with traveling so much. While the first twelve angels were on earth, it was then that they stared mingling with those normal people of earth, breeding angels with man and then showing man the angelic powers that they possessed. They would also give spells to man from heaven, very powerful spells, for fire, wind, and water. These would show them how to use the elements as they needed. They would also be able to move earth.

As time would go on, they would have children, and these children would posses powers also, because they were the angels' offspring. At this time, God and Lucifer had taken notice of what was happening on earth. It made God furious to see all that had been done. So He told the twelve that they would stay on earth and could not come back to heaven or leave the earth. Then as God and Lucifer were wrapping up their fight, more angels wanted to leave heaven. They were siding with Lucifer, so God allowed Lucifer only five hundred angels he could take with him. It was a deal after fighting so much God had made with Lucifer, that he could reign on the earth and the twelve would rule the elements and answer to Lucifer. The five hundred that left heaven were also to be under Lucifer's control. God would give Lucifer orders that he would give to the twelve gods to carry out, but Lucifer would be over all the fallen angels. Once God had shut the door to heaven, He said that they could never return, but be destroyed at the end of time. The twelve gods could and did appear before man at this time. It was when Jesus Christ was born that they could no longer appear before man. If they did appear before man, they would be destroyed.

When the twelve angels came from heaven, God had shut the door and said that no more could leave heaven, or they would be destroyed. So after all the angels that were going to leave heaven left, there was one that came down to earth after God had said no more.

Once the angel arrived on earth, he came to the twelve gods, and they told him to go back to heaven or God will destroy him. It was not shortly after telling him this that God destroyed him. This was done for all to see. He was destroyed right in front of their eyes. This was definitely an example of what happens when you disobey God.

Angels from heaven…where are they? Well, they are all around us. Did you know that everyone is born with their own personal guardian angel? It is true. God has given us our very own guardian angel from birth. This angel protects us during our life. We can also speak to our guardian angels. Some people have more than one with them. If we listen, we can hear them speak to us at times. There are several different types of angels, all with different jobs from God to do. The word *angel* itself means "messenger." We can see in the Bible that God used these angels several times. Gabriel delivered the message to Mary, mother of Jesus. He told her that she was about to be with child, and there are other messages delivered by this archangel.

There are four archangels. The four are Michael, Gabriel, Uriel, and Raphael, each of them with a different job to do also. There are also seraphim, which are high-ranking angels. These angels are directly under God. Then there is the death angel; she is the color blue. Her name is Azreal. This angel will appear to those that are dying, offering them one last chance to believe in Jesus Christ. If the person should choose not to believe and accept this final offer, the person will go to hell.

God has allowed me to speak with several angels. I was able to conduct an interview. They were guests in my house. I assure you that these angels are real, and their stories are straight from them. They will tell us about their jobs that God has given to them. They will tell us a little about heaven, as describing it. Please enjoy the stories that you are about to read. I think these things will shed some light on how we perceive angels and heaven.

God created me as a warrior to do battle for Him. I have many armies that are under me. I do battle against Lucifer and his armies. I am Michael, the archangel. I live in heaven, up in a high place. When God calls me, I go to where I am needed. When I am called to fight battles that Lucifer caused that he was not to start. Sometimes there are many battles a day, and sometimes days without any. Lucifer makes battle with God when he is mad at Him.Sometimes people say that I do things that I don't. People pray to me and believe that I am like a god. People make statues of me, which are false gods, which is wrong.

I have many warriors in heaven and on earth that I command. The warriors on earth let me know when Lucifer is creating battles that he should not. The battles that you don't hear about, I stopped. Sometimes it is just one person that is the battle.

The fallen angels that left heaven, the twelve, will be given a chance to go back to heaven just before the battle of Armageddon.

I have appeared to only a few on earth, those warriors that are dying from battles.

It was I who told the Virgin Mary when she was going to die. I told her within five minutes of her time to die. Mary was forty-one years old at her time of passing. There were more battles after Christ was born. Lucifer had to diminish Christ.

I'm a messenger angel. My name is Melina. When God calls me, He sings our names, and that is how I know He wants to speak to me. We listen, and He tells us to deliver messages to people on earth. Sometimes I appear in spirit to people that are dying. These are only for those going to heaven, and not everybody will receive a message. I deliver warnings, also of happiness. For instance, on the day of 9/11, angels delivered messages of warnings to some of those that were to get on the plane that would later crash. Some listened, and some didn't. These messages happen every day for people not to go somewhere. These are warnings from angels. Sometimes I get to deliver good news to people. I would deliver messages to people to let people know that their loved one is in heaven. A few days ago, I delivered a message to a mother about her child, that she was okay. She was far away in a different country.

My height is about five feet two inches. I have short hair to my shoulders. We wear a white gown or different color sometimes. Sometimes I deliver up to five messages a day, and sometimes none. When I am not delivering messages, I clean in heaven, or just put things back in their place to keep organized.

There are many messenger angels in heaven. They take up the whole left backside of heaven.

People react differently. Those dying believe and are grateful for the messages. Some ask if I am from heaven or hell. Some people call others. These people are the ones that must be convinced, and they tell the other people that they have an angel with them.

Sometimes God has me deliver a message to the preacher in the churches for their Sunday morning service, or God will deliver the message Himself. I only speak one language, but everybody will hear in their language. I travel to deliver messages anywhere on earth.

I am a guardian angel. My name is Lee. I'm about two feet tall, and this is as tall as I can get. I can become three feet tall. I can use an out-of-body voice.

We wait for someone to be born or someone to call for more angels, and God will send us. Assignment is from birth until death. Guardian angels do not deliver messages. I'm twelve thousand years old. I was Princess Anna's guardian.

In heaven, all angels that are guardians like to play in heaven's pools. Heaven is very light and fluffy. There is no darkness ever. You can always see where you are going. There are unique places in heaven that do not exist on earth, like grass that never needs to be cut.

There is a spot in heaven for babies that have died. These babies never cry. These babies will always be babies. These are the babies that never got a chance to breathe their first breath. These are the miscarriages and the babies that no one wanted, babies that were aborted.

Heaven is such a beautiful place. A large side is dedicated to the guardian angels, constantly being assigned. We make an interesting sound while in heaven. We can't make it here on earth. We miss that sound while here on earth. The sound is like that of a hummingbird mixed with the sound of a purring cat.

My favorite part about guarding humans is the way they smell. As an angel, we smell the same. I like that humans can smell differently every day. When I'm in heaven, I miss that smell. Humans are identified by smell. There is food in heaven, only certain places for the humans.

I am the angel of death, Azreal. For spiritual people, when they are dying, I will go to them and inform them that they are dying, that they will be dead in a few minutes. I often tell them they must ask for forgiveness one last time. Sometimes I must tell them to ask for forgiveness of a secret sin, or one that they have forgot about. I tell them that if they listen to me, they get to go to heaven, and if they don't, I wish them well.

So many people I give warnings to avoid death. I cleanse after death; death likes to linger. Death is from Lucifer, and I make sure it doesn't go on to another person.

I am not at everybody's death. I go to the ones who may still have a chance left to get to heaven.

I am the only blue angel that God has ever made.

I love being God's messenger. I am Gabriel, the archangel. The first message I delivered was to the gods from God. The message was directed to all of them. I have been bringing messages down from heaven ever since for God. I am one of the few angels that can speak directly to God. I have seen God. I must look through a veil of light. I carry the veil so I may speak to God. When I see God, I see a giant man on a giant mountain. I see God sitting on a mountain. He is a little smaller than the mountain. God is similar to the look of Christ depicted in Isaiah in the Bible. He looks as an old man with a beard. He wants his messages to be very clear. That's why I can see Him. I very much enjoy my job.

When God told me the message I had to deliver to Mary, I couldn't believe that He was finally sending His Son. I told Him, "You will have to expand heaven because more people will be here."

He said, "First, they must believe, and you do not know the humans that well."

I took the message to Mary one night. She believed me right away. She was not shocked nor surprised as you might think. She was very happy. She was crying, and she was just fifteen years old. So she [Mary] was only fifteen years old when she was pregnant. I told her not to worry about her family, I will speak to them. When I left her, she said that she would accept this gift. When I left, her she was crying. So I went to God and told Him about her response. God then gave me the message to give to her family. So I went and delivered the message the next night. After that, we spent much time rejoicing in heaven.

One of the most important things about delivering my messages, I think, is that they change the course of the world. I am very excited to bring the world what will be my last message. This will be a message that everyone will hear, no matter where you are. This will be the sounding of the trumpet of God, announcing Christ's return. Although this will be a very exciting thing to do, delivering this message, it will also bring very much pain for a short while. I am excited to wait for the exact message from God, because after the trumpet sounds, there will be words that I will speak that everyone will hear. After the last message, my plans are unknown. I believe I will still be God's messenger, but to whom, I do not know.

I bring the light of God to people in troubled times. I am Uriel, the archangel. I like to rescue people that God has chosen. I have not done a lot of work recently, but I did do a lot of work when Jesus was on earth. I was one of His protectors. I was with Mary at conception and with Jesus to the cross. I protected Mary and Joseph from ridicule and danger, and I helped them flee when needed. I rescued some men and donkeys when Jesus needed to cross a river because the river filled faster than they thought. I was with Jesus His whole life. I helped many babies, children, women, and workers in 9/11 [the rescuers].

There was a prison in northern France in WWII that was a Nazi prison holding women and children only. There was a woman in there. Her name was Lena. Her prayers were answered by God. She and her child did not die in the prison. God sent me there, and I released everyone there to freedom safely. Lena was a true believer. She prayed, and God answered and saved everyone.

Sometimes I go to a church when it is full of people. I touch the crowd of people. I touch each one on their head and some maybe twice, I like to go to churches when I hear people call who have a strong belief so the church or ones persons call, that a strong belief, and that's where I would go.

When God calls me and needs me, I go before Him. Mount Zion is the mountain that God sits upon, and the earth is His footstool. I bring the light of God to those that are in serious need of God's help. I wear a hat to go before God and speak with Him. It covers my eyes so I may look upon Him. Sometimes I work with Michael to help him in heaven prepare for an upcoming battle. I do recruit for him sometimes too. I recruit for Michael's army by choosing only select few that meet God's qualifications, such as how obedient the angels are, and for man, it is how obedient they were on earth. Then they go through training from now until the end.

As a Christian, you will know who the Antichrist is. The Antichrist will come on the scene before the rapture [Christ's return] takes place. Then soon after his appearance and he announces himself as Christ, then the true Jesus Christ will return. So all the true believers will know the true Christ as the Bible has taught us. Beware of false prophets.

I stand behind God. I can throw God's anger to people from heaven. I don't have much of a job till Christ comes back. I am the archangel Raphael.

The last time I came from heaven was before Jesus, and the reason was to prepare some people [key figures] that would help prepare His way, people that had to play out the stories to prepare for His coming.

For instance, Noah. God came to Noah once then. It was I that walked him through building the ark. Step by step I would stay with him, also with his wife and other men that joined him on the boat. I helped keep their concentration and determination. There was a small man named Tobia. He had a special job he had to do for God, so I stayed with him until it was done, a Jewish man. He delivered fruit to the wealthy people. Soon he started to deliver messages as well as fruit. In this, I helped him also. He would deliver messages to help others believe in Jesus's coming.

I did a lot of secret things for God. I was there for the destruction, and it was I that destroyed Sodom and Gomorrah. Before it was destroyed, I delivered warnings.

My job is to bring the message and as many souls that will come to Christ during the tribulation period. They will only get to heaven at that time by works, belief, and many sacrifices, including their own death possibly. The sacrifices will be of great pain and causing great pain and unimaginable sacrifices. I want people to know and understand that hell is real and will never go away. Don't doubt that God will put you there for your sins. I hope that I never have to leave any messages to anyone who reads this, for if I do, you will be sacrificing much.

I am Seraphiel, a seraphim angel. I was created about three thousand years after Lucifer. I worked alongside Lucifer in heaven for many years.

My main job before there were people was to keep angels in check and report problems or ideas to God. After there were people, my job was to take care of people or certain people. Some people like John the Baptist, Mary, Philip, and a couple of people today.

I can never appear in my natural form, or man would burn up in my sight. There are four seraphim: one's fallen [Lucifer], myself, and others that go unnamed. We are God's highest creation and most powerful of angels. I can create anger in a person for the better of God's will.

David asked for a title for this book that he would write, and I gave him *A Guest in My House*.

I have been alive for about ten thousand years. My name is NeTee. I am a messenger angel from God. God uses me because I can hold great secrets. I'm a newer angel, and everyone loves me. The other day, two other angels moved out of my way to give me their seats. I really enjoy coming down from heaven. I am very glad that I get to speak to you.

When called upon, either God sends me or one of the angels with you will call on me. I have been a messenger angel to Peter. I gave him several messages. I told him where to hide his writings [scriptures]. I also delivered a message to Queen Ann of Russia. My message to her was to get out of the city, because her sister was going to kill her, because she was mad at her [eighteenth century].

I would tell everyone a message: You really want to go to heaven! It is beautiful!

Angels are real. They are all around us, from guardian to arch. They all have wonderful jobs to do for God. What I think is great is the fact that we can talk to them, and they hear us. If we listen, we can hear them and their messages from God. We also should listen to that still small voice. That would be God talking to us. Learn to listen.

So many times I have felt a presence like no other. It would be so comforting and uplifting to me. That would be the spirit of God. Angels also give a presence different than an earthbound spirit. You do know that God sends His angels to comfort us in time of need. They are always there and are only a prayer away. If we feel we need more angels to help or comfort us, we just need to ask God to send more angels to us, and He will.

Since I interviewed the gods, I have learned so much by talking to them more. I learned that they can materialize, but not in front of any person. They eat just as we do and sleep, needing rest also. They meet at Mt. Ararat, have meetings, and some live there. They say Zeus keeps it seventy-five degrees and sunny. God at times will attend their meeting, giving them instructions on what is needed by God to be done. Lucifer also will attend some of these meetings.

These gods can possess a human body. The movie *The Exorcist* was based on a true story about a boy that was possessed by a demon. The spirit that did possess that boy was Ares, one of the Greek gods. Ares is the one fallen angel (Greek god) that will possess, and it becomes terrible for the person he possesses. He stayed with the boy for a long time. It took a long time to free the boy from Ares. The other goddess and gods like to possess for sex. These are called incubus and succubus. They will possess a woman or man, and they have sex with the partner of the one that is possessed. It is then that maybe the partner might pick up on the difference in behavior, with the one possessed becoming more aggressive than the person might normally be.

Hestia is also known as the Black Widow. It is she who will possess a woman that is with a man cheating on his wife. If she catches this act, she will kill the male. It is the prayers of those wives that Hestia hears, all crying because they suspect that their husband is cheating on them. When Hestia hears the cry, she will inspect the male by possessing his girlfriend at the time. She will touch his head then see all that has been happening. When she sees him as cheating on his wife, it is then that she will kill. She can bring a knife out of thin air by just calling for it, then uses it to kill. It is only the man that is cheating and has children that he does not think about that Hestia will kill.

Evil spirits can possess, but when they do, they will be sent straight to hell. Evil spirits will cause other spirits to do bad things also, like playing tricks on us by moving things. We thought we placed it there, but now it's moved somewhere else. This was probably moved by an evil spirit. Maybe you have experienced this in your house. Also out-of-body voices—this is another thing. Have you ever thought that someone was calling your name? They were. It was a spirit playing with you. In the middle of the night, you are fast asleep but are then awakened by a voice calling your name, or you heard some things moving around downstairs. It was the spirits that are in your house.

Angels are always with us; we each have a guardian angel. When we need them, they are always there. All we need to do is just call upon them and God for help.

Earthbound spirits are all around us. It is like another world that we can't see with our eyes. No matter what, they exist. These are the spirits that did not go to the light for whatever reason they had. Maybe that spirit felt like they were going to be sent to hell, so they passed up the light, or they thought that they could help by looking after their loved ones. No spirit can do anything for their loved ones; it would have been better for them to go to the light. These same spirits can become evil spirits. They become that way by not listening to the angel's instructions when they passed on.

All our life, we were to make choices. Same in the afterlife. What or where should I do or go? The best choice is to have gone to the light, but if you chose to stay on earth, then there are rules to follow. The things we say and do while we are in these bodies right now have an impact on our lives after death. Did we believe in Jesus Christ, or did we get caught up in religion and lose sight of what was really important? There are so many distractions in life to make us lose our way. So now because we passed up our light when we should have gone to our final resting place, we end up looking for a way to find that light again. We travel all over the world and see everything that we couldn't have seen before, but really no enjoyment comes from it. We can't eat, only smell the great dishes that are being prepared in the kitchens of where we have visited, but then we are quickly reminded that we are no longer living. With no sense of time, things become very boring very fast. We try talking to the living, but no one hears us. We scream, and still no one hears us.

Only very few people can hear the spirits talk. These people have a gift for hearing and sometimes seeing these spirits. These people are sometimes called mediums. It is that once a spirit knows that they can be heard, they will keep coming back to talk with the medium and also tell other spirits of their find. This is very important in the spirit world, because they have so much to say. That is why I decided to connect with the spirit world, to get answers that all the living would love to know, just to answer questions that we all have wanted to know for a very long time.

Is there truly life after death? What is the death experience like? What is that light everyone keeps talking about? Is there a heaven and hell? Will I be able to help my family from the other side? All these questions can be answered in this book, and maybe some other questions that I didn't mention. I say yes to life after death. The light is the way to eternity, a judgment from God that takes us to heaven or hell, all depending on what we did with His Son. Yes, there is a heaven and hell; both are so very real. If it were possible to go to hell and talk with some of them that have been there a while, what do you think they would tell us? I believe they would say, "Please believe in Jesus Christ. He is the way, the truth, and the life. Believe, believe, please believe, and tell my families that this place is real, and I don't want to see them down here." What a horrific message to give to the family, but it's the truth, and the truth does set us free.

As I have spoken to each and every spirit, angel or demon, all as a guest in my house, I gathered as much information as I could in regard to all the questions that might be raised about life after death. I think that each and every one of us truly has an interest in what happens after this life. We go to church, we listen to those who might have had a near-death experience, and we begin to formulate our own ideas in our head as to what life after the grave might be. We all know we have souls that are eternal, but what is life after death really like? I only know one way to find out for sure. That is to ask the dead that walk the earth. These spirits are known as earthbound spirits, and yes, they can hear us talk and understand us. The problem is that we can't hear them. Only very few people can listen and hear what the spirits say. These people are called mediums. A really good, genuine medium will listen and get the true message from the other side. It is then that we can ask our questions that we all want to know and only they can tell. Since interviewing each spirit, I can answer those questions that before I was totally lost on.

Each spirit has given me their own experience with death as only they experienced and can tell you. Every death was different, but the end results were all the same. They all had come to a light that they must pass through to get to heaven, and all were given the same choices to stay on earth or pass on through. A lot of people can speculate, but after you have read this book, it is then you will have a much better understanding of how death and the other side work. I think that the spirits have all explained and have tried to answer our questions as to what they know and understand. The purpose of this book was to enlighten our knowledge and educate us on life after death, what to expect, or just to find out what happens.

I have really enjoyed speaking to all the guests I had in my house. I loved listening to all their stories, all very interesting. I want to thank my medium Faith for working with me as we both heard the spirits talk and write their stories.

If anything, we can learn by the mistakes we'd seen were made and save ourselves the tragedies that we'd seen all these spirits went through. Truly a life-changing experience.

ABOUT THE AUTHOR

My name is David Guddy, and I'm 46 years old. I live in Ohio, and I lived in a haunted house at the time of writing this book. I have had many experiences in that house, also throughout my life, and this is what brought me to pen my experiences. I am a Christian and have tremendous faith in God, that is what got me through writing this book. I think we must know and believe that we are surrounded by spirits, angels, and demons, and if we watch and listen, we are able to hear or see evidence of them.